Man Amongst Gods

Mikael Svanström

Man Amongst Gods

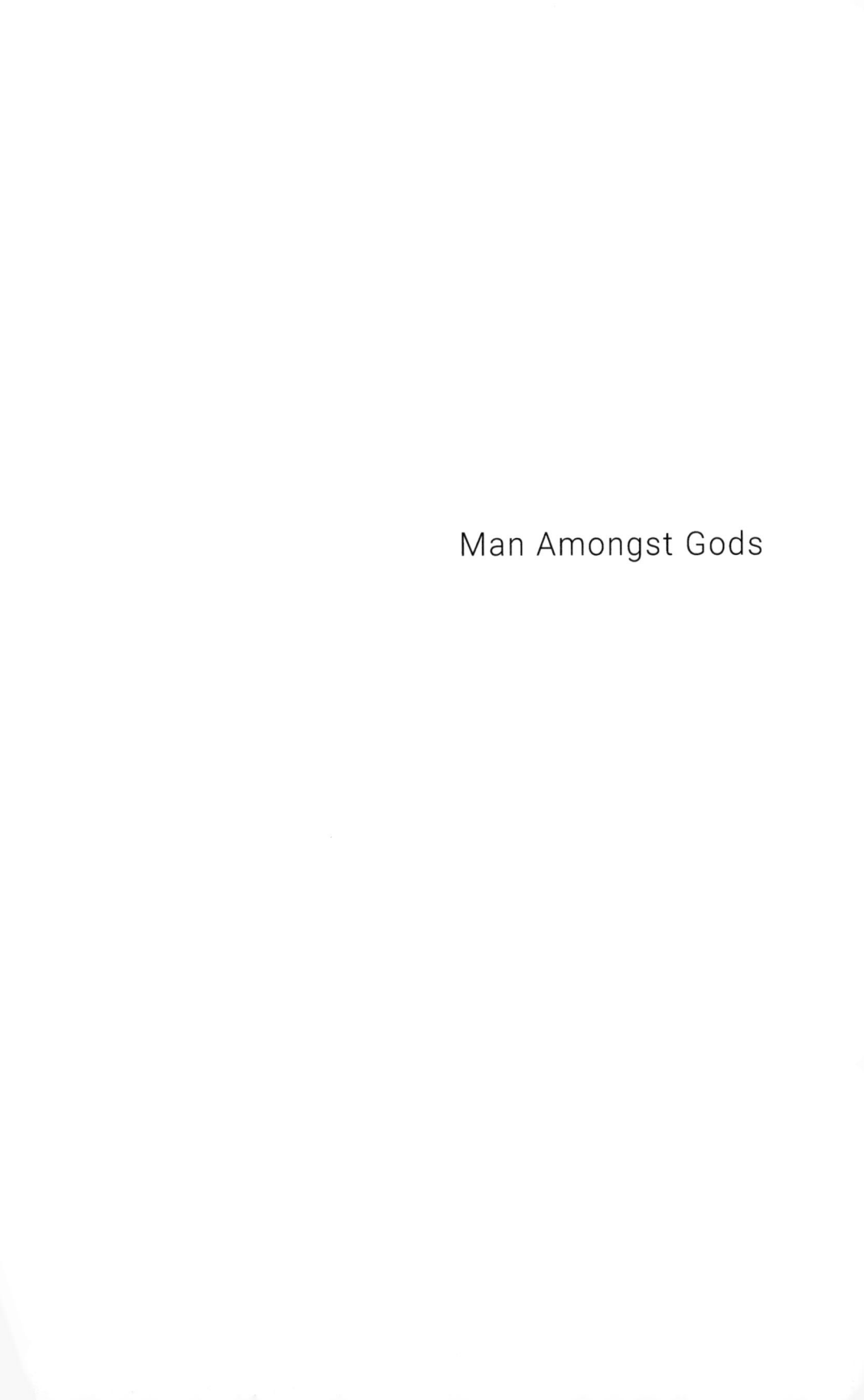

This is a work of fiction. Names, characters, businesses, places, events and incidents are either the products of the author's imagination or used in a fictitious manner. Any resemblance to actual persons, living or dead, or actual events is purely coincidental.

1st Edition
Text copyright © 2024 Mikael Svanström
All Rights Reserved

Edited by: Michael DeAngelo
Cover image: Created by Mikael Svanström using Midjourney v4

To Gerhard Diedricks, Anders Karlsson and Marcus Sigurdsson.
This book wouldn't have been the same without you!

1

Hong Kong Red Zone

"I am Rat, firstborn of the Hong Kong Red Zone, and I claim my land."

She'd climbed Sunset Peak for the first time, the morning sun warming her back. She crouched down, her instinct from fourteen years of hiding, but she soon stood up, arms stretched out as if to embrace what lay before her.

The city spread out below. Giant metal cylinders rose from the earth, reaching towards the heavens. They reminded her of machines designed for some nefarious purpose. Or maybe they were monuments of an age past. How people could live in those was beyond her. How so many people could exist that such housing was necessary was equally baffling.

"Get down, you idiot!"

"What? There is..."

Jason pulled her down and pointed. At first, she saw only the low-growing vegetation and a few low-flying birds. Then one bush shifted and another in an unmistakable line towards them.

"Run!"

"We won't make it."

"We have to try!"

They ran down the narrow, barely visible path they had used to make their ascent. The bushes clawed at their legs as they stormed by. Rat hazarded a look behind. She caught a momentary glimpse of the machine hunting them; a five-legged spider, with three metal cords rising from its small torso swaying back and forth. It sped down the mountainside in pursuit. It was an old Scout model, and she hoped it no longer had functional ranged capabilities. If it did, they'd soon know.

"We're not gonna make it," Rat shouted to Jason, who was just a few metres ahead. "It's corrupted, for sure."

"So, there won't be any others," Jason shouted over his shoulder. "We should split up."

Rat knew Jason was right. There was no way they'd escape without weapons, so splitting up ensured one of them would survive.

She veered off the path to the left, hoping the Scout would choose the easier route and chase Jason. But Jason had the same idea and left the trail in the other direction.

Scrap! She was dead, for sure!

The Scout's logic was basic when on its own. Unless it had a specific target, it would chase whomever it was most likely to catch. There was no way to make her the less desirable target, so she sped up, knowing every step threatened to send her sprawling. Behind her, the clawed metal feet scraped against the rock as it increased speed to catch up. It hadn't used any ranged weapons, suggesting they were no longer functional. A small win, but still she ran.

She scanned her surroundings for an escape route, but she knew the machine behind her could follow her wherever she went. She didn't need to check to know it was catching up. The hillside became steeper, turning from a slope to a cliff. Below was a dense undergrowth with sporadic groups of taller trees almost reaching the height of the cliff. She hazarded another look behind. The Scout was only meters away, the metal cords stretching towards her.

A split-second decision born more from instinctual survival than anything else, had her veer to the left towards the cliff and jump. She was suspended in mid-air, imagining metal pincers ready to pierce her back. Gravity had not yet reclaimed her. The adrenaline pumping through her system made her hyper-aware of her surroundings. The leaves on the large tree still had water pooling from the morning dew. Light refracted from the almost circular droplets painting the leaves in ever-shifting colours. In that frozen moment, she was free, unburdened by any concerns for the future. She may live or die, but it was out of her hands now.

Time restarted as her momentum caused her to slam face-first into the top of the tree. It swayed from her weight as she desperately clung to it, threatening to break at any moment. Her peripheral vision caught the Scout standing on the edge, retracting its pincers. It was a second-generation Scout with a stun mechanism that reached at least five metres. It was closer than that now. It could have other ranged weapons as modifications, but it would have used them by now. Its logic demanded her capture, but it wouldn't damage itself to reach its goal. At least, that was its original programming. The corrupted Scouts could be unpredictable.

She felt herself slipping. The wet leaves were an ever-changing surface, resisting her desperate attempts to hang on.

The Scout reached towards her. If it jumped, it would get her for sure. She steeled herself, ready for the impact of the cold metal clinging to her back, but a few moments passed without instant death, so she glanced back.

It was gone!

She slid down the trunk to the ground and set off. She wasn't supposed to return to the settlement immediately. There were designated routes that were especially difficult for machines to traverse, but she didn't have time for that. She knew Jason wouldn't be able to evade it. He was fast, but only for short sprints. It would track him down and catch him within minutes.

His only chance would be how quickly she could return to the settlement for help. If luck remained on her side, Tann would be there and willing to help, even if he seldom took part in excursions nowadays.

2

Hunted Scout

Tann had always liked this settlement site. It was relatively hidden and far enough away from any Red Zone for stray machines to be uncommon. There was enough to eat, especially now at the end of summer when the fruit on the Rapple trees was ripe. The sweet scent of the fruit lingered in the air, promising a record harvest. He hoped they could remain here for the next three months, longer than they had ever spent in one location since the tribe had formed almost twenty years ago. Machine attacks were less and less frequent and when they occurred, it was a usually a stray, corrupted Scout, not the coordinated strikes in the past that could easily wipe out an entire tribe. Why things had changed was anyone's guess. Maybe it wasn't worth hunting down humans any longer. Maybe the AI had grown tired of its old games and focused on exterminating the posthumans instead. He didn't know and he didn't much care. The survival of the tribe was all that mattered.

"Boss?"

"Huh?" Tann looked over at Sandrine, his second in command, who nodded towards the man in front of them. She was slender and of average height, not that Tann thought of her that way. In his mind she towered over everyone else. She was ten years his junior and better than him in all things that mattered. He was sure she'd take over when he was no longer up to the job of keeping the tribe safe.

"The camp," Sandrine said, raising an eyebrow. "It is ready for inspection."

She nodded towards Xuwei, who'd been responsible for setting up the camp now for the past three years. He was the opposite of Sandrine. Muscular and tall, always in work clothes ready to lend a hand in the running of the camp. The inspection was a formality. Tann had long ago lost track of the intricacies of establishing and running the infrastructure of the camp and relied completely on Xuwei and his team. As a result, he doubted he'd find any issues. Xuwei had perfected the layout and positioning of the aerogel insulated, 3D graphene collapsible huts that served as their housing.

Xuwei guided them through the camp, calling attention to minor upgrades and changes he'd made since last changeover. It wasn't much, but that was a good thing.

"I've laid out the huts in a semi-circle with the main hall on the other side. We're closer to the water this time and I've introduced modifications to the dismantling process. It should save us almost five minutes when we break camp."

"And if attacked?" Sandrine asked.

"No change there. Shorter distance to reach the boats, but that's about it."

Tann nodded. He wasn't really paying attention. Sandrine would call out any issues. Lately the future of the tribe, and maybe even humankind if there even was such a thing, had been on his mind. He didn't know how many humans remained. The Eight Plague wiped out all major population centres across the world. The few survivors that were unaffected by the posthuman virus gathered in tribes to survive. A year later, machines appeared designed to hunt and neutralise humans. They attacked any permanent settlement. He knew of five other nomadic tribes remaining in this part of the world. They kept their contact to a minimum, only sending quick bursts as all communication channels were monitored and anything longer could be traced back to its origin.

"We've had to print additional parts for the organic recyclers. I've located them together with the solar cells in an open area closer to the beach."

Xuwei continued the walkthrough. Tann wandered along with them, nodding now and then to give the appearance of participation. These ceremonies had kept them alive for a long time. Tann had been the instigator of many and knew how important they were. Still, he found his mind wandering.

Rat appeared at full speed, careering through the camp, almost colliding with them in her hurry to get away from an unseen threat.

"Rat! What's the hurry?" Tann scanned the forest line where he'd first seen her. Rat was always up to something. Tann had many times predicted she wouldn't see her fifteenth birthday, which was only days away.

She halted. Her slender body twirled on the spot; blue bright eyes firmly fixated on the spot she'd come from. A fresh gash trickled blood across her shoulder.

"Scout!" she gasped between shallow breaths. "Corrupted."

Tann nodded. She'd given them the most valuable pieces of information first. A corrupted Scout they could deal with. There was no reason to break camp if they could find and disable it.

"How many?" Sandrine asked. "Just one?"

Rat nodded so fiercely sweat droplets flew from her short black hair, like a dog shaking itself after getting wet.

"Let's go," Tann said, smiling grimly.

"You're coming?" Sandrine said.

Tann noticed the slight narrowing of her eyes, just a hint of disapproval. She was right. He was the leader of the tribe. Going after a Scout could be dangerous, and risking his life unnecessarily wasn't in the best interest of the tribe. He shrugged in response.

"I didn't say anything," Sandrine objected.

"You didn't have to."

"I better go too then, just to make sure you don't get into any trouble. You want it captured?"

Tann shook his head.

"Good," she replied and yelled for two tribe members to join them.

"You lead the way," Tann said to Rat.

She nodded and headed off the way she'd come, weaving through the lush palms, moving leaves aside as she went. At the outset, Tann found it hard to keep up. He remembered giving her the nickname that had stuck so many years ago. She'd been small and slender, able to get through the smallest crevice as if it wasn't there. She was always scraped and bruised from her latest exploits, gathering items from a bygone era that no one seemed willing to discuss, as if it was an embarrassment. Tann liked her. She may have been reckless, but the tribe's survival depended on people like her.

"You left with Jason earlier," Sandrine said. A statement, not a question. "On one of your scavenging hunts, I assume?"

This was why Sandrine was so much better than him. He should have known that, but he didn't.

"No," Rat responded, eyes downcast. "I just wanted to see the city and the giant cylinder-things people lived in."

"And where is Jason now?" Sandrine asked, steel in her voice.

"I don't know. We split up. It came after me."

"What?" Tann said. "You outran a Scout?"

"I jumped," she said, shrugging her shoulders as if that explained everything.

They continued their trek, half-running, trading speed for safety, out of the undergrowth, up the hill, and along the ridge as they neared Sunset Peak. They had to find the Scout before it disappeared and reported its discovery to other machines.

"You lost it here?"

Tann eyed the distance between the edge and the tree. There was no question how she'd escaped. Bright red smears stood like beacons on the large green leaves. He doubted he'd make that jump, or even attempt it.

But Jason and Rat had followed their training. They wouldn't survive a fight, so they separated, minimising the number of targets it could pursue and capture. Whoever the Scout pursued would perish, but become a worthy sacrifice, allowing others to survive. This time the chosen prey had escaped, and the only logical choice was to locate the other target.

Rat nodded.

"And Jason? Where did he go?"

Rat pointed down the other side of the ridge, and they ran. Tann hoped it wasn't too late. They'd spied machines in this area before and usually gave it a wide berth, not wanting strays to follow them back to the settlement area.

They didn't have to run far. The Scout was dragging Jason down the mountainside. For a moment Tann thought the boy could still be alive, that the Scout was following its original programming, but his unseeing eyes stared into the rising sun, and his limbs sagged like a rag doll as the machine dragged him along the ground.

At least it hadn't reached any other machines—not yet. Tann studied the small Scout. A spider-legged base model, modified to the point the only thing that remained was the chassis. Corrupted Scouts scavenged technology from other machines to replace old, broken parts. He'd seen this model before a long time ago. It wasn't long after the Eight Plague. Machines just like this one attacked the first tribe he'd joined. Scouts swarmed from all sides, like bugs uncovered from under a rock. They were the initial attack, with two major weapons at their disposal: a fast-acting non-lethal neuro toxin, with injectors at the end of metal cords that rose from its body, swaying like rattle snakes; and an electric charge delivered from a small taser with a five-metre range. Their purpose was to incapacitate as many people as possible without killing them, usually targeting a specific group of people. They came fast, relying on speed, surprise, and fear. What came after was worse. Much worse.

"Tann?" Sandrine asked, elbowing him in the side. He didn't need to glance her way to know what she thought. He could hear the frustration from that single word.

"Just deciding what to do," he said and began doing just that. They had long since abandoned using normal guns against Scout models. They were too fast, almost impossible to hit. Instead, they used cruder weapons, limiting their movement before disposing of them with a blunt weapon.

Through the years they'd experimented with electricity, limited EMP bursts and explosives. They had even tried water to short-circuit their wiring with limited success. Acids reacted to slow and became a danger to the people when the machines attacked them. Trapping their limbs had proven the most successful method of disabling them.

Tann retrieved a foam grenade from a pouch on his belt. They didn't have many left and he'd hoped not to use it, but the Scout had already killed one of them. They couldn't risk another casualty.

He lobbed the grenade in a high arc, dropping on the machine from above. It activated on impact. A mushroom of white foam exploded with a five-metre radius coating the Scout and everything around it.

The foam solidified to a gluelike substance, fusing to anything it touched. Strands of rubbery, sticky material restricted the machine's movements until it could no longer move forward. The rubber tendrils stretched, but immediately snapped back.

They waited twenty seconds for the fusing reaction to complete. The Scout lay on its side, unable to right itself. The old servo engines whined in protest as it kept resisting the haphazard restraints. Tann was relieved to find that the Scout didn't have functioning communication devices. There was no reason to suspect it was anything but a stray robot wandering randomly, hunting for other machines to cannibalise.

"What's wrong?" Sandrine asked as she lodged her knife into the undercarriage of the Scout, twisting it open.

"What do you mean?"

"You've checked out. Been more than a month now. I don't care, but it is affecting the tribe."

Tann remained silent, refusing to acknowledge the obvious truth in her words.

"I will contest your leadership in tonight's tribe meeting," she continued. Tann saw Rat listening to their conversation, her eyes widening as Sandrine spoke.

"You do what you have to do," Tann replied.

3

Birth

As they returned to the village, navigating the traps they had set up around the perimeter, a young woman, Mo Chou, approached them.

"What fresh hell might this be?" Tann said quietly to himself.

"Jodi is giving birth," Sandrine said. "You know that. Or you should know that."

He had been aware, but somehow even that, the most important event there was, had somehow slipped his mind.

"It is time," Mo Chou said. She was twenty years old, born only days after the Plague hit. One of the lucky few young children that survived the slaughter of the first few years. No one knew how many humans had survived the initial attack and the plague, but everyone agreed most of the survivor were captured or killed in the three years after that.

She'd once told Tann her name meant "free of sadness". The irony of a name like that was hard to ignore. She was a fierce fighter when needed, hardened by years of escaping death. Sadness was imbued in her, an integral part channelled into everything she did.

"Lead the way," Tann said.

"The birth was uneventful. A healthy boy. 3.6 kilos. 50 centimetres. All vitals normal."

Tann waited. Healthy was fine, but not enough.

"I've taken a swab already. It was inconclusive, so we are doing a blood test. We're waiting for the results now. This is her third, so maybe this time."

Tann nodded. They were no longer hunted down and killed by the machines, but it didn't matter. The virus turning people into posthumans remained. He'd been responsible for that, though at the time he hadn't realised how the dominoes would fall. It was no longer as potent as the original strain, but from data shared between nearby tribes, the infection rate was still around fifty percent. No one knew why the virus remained, since they were all infected a long time ago. Maybe animals carried it, or they were all carriers once infected, even if it didn't trigger the change. It didn't matter. It was a fact of life, like the posthumans and the machines.

They entered Jodi's hut. She was on the bed, cradling the unnamed newborn in her arms. Her dark hair lay plastered against her skin. She looked up, eyes darting between them for a second, then her focus returned to the baby.

Mo Chou held a small device up to the light, peering at the small screen. She shook her head before her arms dropped to her sides.

Jodi wailed, her arms tightening around the baby boy like a shield against the world around her. "I'm not leaving him! I'm not!"

Her protestations stopped abruptly as she stared at something behind him. A slight variation in the flow of air in the room had already alerted Tann to the figure entering the hut. He was sure others waited outside. The figure was naked and hairless, skin grey and patterned like a snake. The posthumans had specialized much like bees in a hive. This one, and the ones outside, were specialised for physical tasks, even violence if needed. It was human in appearance, but something was wrong, as if its proportions were slightly off. Wiry muscles wrapped like cords up its elongated legs and arms. Tann had seen posthumans take on machines without weapons and win, an impossibility for a normal human being.

The posthuman reached the side of the bed and held out its hands. It remained like that as Jodi's eyes again darted between Sandrine, Tann and Mo Chou.

Jodi clasped the baby tightly to her chest. "You can't let them take him!"

"We can't raise one of them," Sandrine said. "You know that. It will leave us as soon as it can."

Tann nodded. Early on, they had tried to hide the newborn posthumans, usually on the insistence of the parents. Tann saw the usefulness of this too. If they could raise a posthuman child, maybe it could help them in their dealings with this strange race. It hadn't worked. As soon as the child was mobile, it went in search of others like themselves.

"You have to," Tann said. "It isn't one of us."

Tears streamed down her face. She gently touched the side of her baby boy's face. His eyes popped open. She stared into his dark brown eyes. Tann was close enough to see what she saw. The infant's stare fixed on his mother's face for a second, and then darted off to examine the room, settling on the posthuman standing next to the bed. It reached out, not to his mother, but to this alien creature still waiting with arms outstretched.

Jodi sneered and almost brusquely pushed the baby into the waiting arms.

"Take it! It is no child of mine!"

The posthuman cradled the child gently, the skin of its hands and arms melding around the child's form, and it turned to leave. It focused on Tann for an instance.

"No more breeding," it said. "No more of this randomised mess. We will assimilate it into the hive."

Tann had heard it said before, but never asked what it meant. Assimilation into the hive sounded too much like death.

* * *

Death hadn't finished with them that day, Tann thought grimly as he watched Jodi's body sway from the tree branch. He should have seen it coming. Three babies taken from her in the past five years. Three failures building on top of each other, high enough for her to reach the noose and place it around her weary neck.

It had been a grim day for the tribe. Two dead and a baby no longer with them. The tribe no longer grew from survivors joining them, and there weren't enough human children born to replace those who died. He suspected other tribes were experiencing the same decline.

He sat down on the floor with an old Omni in his hand. Wires snaked out to the solar cells on the roof. The battery had long since stopped working. The networked world remained, but it was a dangerous place for human minds. Machines hunted them in the physical world and virtual agents hunted them online. No one even attempted jacking into the network any longer. The two-way neural interface was an invitation for a virtual agent to infect the brain and try to rewire it, usually with fatal results.

An Omni could still connect, but even this had its dangers. The connection itself was a beacon for any Scouts scouring the physical world.

The Omni's cracked black screen came to life, displaying a keyboard and a basic messaging application. This was the only reason he used it. Tann had designed the messaging application himself, ensuring it minimised connectivity. It sent the smallest package possible synchronously. And because it was point to point, both sides had to be connected at the same time. If communication was text only, he was confident it would avoid detection. Still, they kept their conversations short.

A message appeared from Haoyu, leader of a tribe in the same region. Tann was happy for the distraction.

Haoyu: TikTak!
Tann: Really?

Tann had told Haoyu about his past as a hacker and his old avatar name. Back then, it was the only name he'd respond to. Now it seemed quaint, like a mildly embarrassing childhood nickname.

Haoyu: I thought I'd set the scene.
Tann: You're making no sense. How's the tribe?
Haoyu: Still stationary. 3 months now. You?
Tann: Moved yesterday. 2 dead. 1 baby lost.
Haoyu: Their stories have ended. Ours have not.

Tann nodded to himself. Haoyu was right. They had to move on. Mankind's survival depended on them, whatever tragedies they had to suffer to achieve it.

Haoyu: I have a surprise.
Tann: What?
Haoyu: A memory stick. We've found one.
Tann: A memory stick? You mean a memTag?

memTag. Tann said the word out loud. It sounded strange to his ears. A word from a different age that only held relevance in its own time.

Haoyu: Call it what you want. We don't know what to do with it. It is encrypted.
Tann: Throw it away then.
Haoyu: There is a plain message on it too. You can read it with an old Omni.
Tann: And?

Tann wondered why Haoyu was interested in this. Not that this was the first time. He frequently dug up old tech he wanted to use from the outskirts of Red Zones.

Haoyu: You spoke of a posthuman you knew years ago. Tom Devine.
Tann: I should never have told you.

Haoyu: Well, now it came in useful.
Tann: Ok, I'm interested. What does it say?
Haoyu: It ends with "To Tom Devine, with love."
Tann: Really? I don't believe you.
Haoyu: That's what it says. And it is recent. A year or two at the most.
Tann: Can you send it to me?
Haoyu: I can send the plain text part. The rest is too big to send with this crappy app you made.

The message came as a small text attachment.

It is time we end this. Hopefully this will find you before it is too late. If you are half as smart as you think, you'll work out the encryption key from the first place we met.
He won't though.
To Tom Devine, with love

Tann: Is that it? It doesn't even make sense. What's with the second line? "He won't though." It doesn't add up.
Haoyu: That's why I sent it to you. I have no idea what it means! Figured you might.

It was so random, so strange. It had to mean something. He paced back and forth in the small hut, mind racing. Survival of the tribe had been his life, but there was a bigger picture. The day's events had forced him to accept the tribe was slowly dying. Maybe this message, however incoherent, showed the way to a solution. It was a longshot, but why did it exist in the first place? He had to know.

Tann: I'll come and get it.
Haoyu: You'll come? I can send someone.
Tann: No. I'll come.

Haoyu: You know where we are. We'll be swapping camp soon, so hurry.

Tann: Will do.

Tann disconnected the Omni and immediately packed a bag.

"Going somewhere?" Sandrine stood in the doorway.

"I need to deal with something."

"Something that can help the tribe?"

"Possibly."

"You're not just running away?"

"Possibly."

Sandrine shook her head and closed the distance between them with a few quick steps. Tann instinctively raised his hands, ready to fend off an attack if it came, but she just embraced him. She could still surprise him, even after all this time.

"Go," she said. "You're no good here anyway."

He was about to protest, but she was right. His immediate decision to leave had many contributing factors, one of them the tribal meeting this evening.

"I'll deal with things here. Just go."

4

An Unwanted Companion

Rat watched as Tann left the village unannounced. It wasn't as if he was prohibited from leaving, but his body language suggested subterfuge. She'd made it a habit to keep track of Tann whenever her duties allowed. He fascinated her. The stories told of Tann bordered on legends. He'd risen to leader of the tribe over ten years ago and saved them from extinction more than once. It was as if he instinctively understood the machines better than anyone else. What they'd do. Where they'd hunt. How they'd attack. And he used this skill to find the best locations to settle, how to set up perimeter defences, how to escape when needed. Rumour had it he'd been involved in the Plague somehow, but she didn't know how. Not that it mattered. Ancient history, however fascinating, was pointless. It changed nothing.

He'd been sending messages to the other tribe leaders just before he left. She'd seen him preparing an old screen to connect to the forbidden network. This was more interesting. One of her pack mates had told her you could use it to talk to anyone in the world! She couldn't comprehend this. Wouldn't all this shouting back and forth across enormous distances make it impossible to understand what the others were saying? The practical technology of the past was fascinating—especially the weapons—but she struggled to understand the purpose of what Tann called information technology. But anything forbidden was bound to be interesting. And seeing Tann skulking out of the settlement was exactly that. Maybe she didn't understand the why, but she knew it would be exciting.

There was no rule preventing her from following Tann to ensure his safety. She was doing him a favour really, as one rule stated they shouldn't leave camp alone. She smiled to herself, pleased to have conjured an explanation based on the rules she so often ignored.

Tann had already disappeared. Rat scanned her surroundings, ensured no one paid her any attention, and followed.

Three hours later and Tann showed no sign of reaching any kind of destination. Quite the contrary. He'd navigated the serpentine roads across the island until reaching one of the main roads leading towards the Red Zone. This was further from this settlement than she'd ever been before.

She was also acutely aware the point of no return was rapidly approaching. They could still return to the settlement before sunset, but this was pushing it. What was so important he broke all his own rules?

This wasn't even a decision. Her want to know Tann's destination far outweighed her want to return to the tribe and her chores. This was a real adventure! And who knew? She might even help him in the quest of his.

Tann continued his trek along the wide, empty road. The scale of everything in the old world was incomprehensible. What could be so important that you needed four lanes each way to get to and from it? Their lives were so busy, but why?

Only the innermost lanes remained now, vegetation kept at bay somehow. She assumed machines used it still, but so far, she hadn't seen any. According to the stories, vehicles to transport humans were all cleared from the roads, the materials used to create new machines.

Rat followed Tann on the other side of the median strip, leaving as much distance as she dared. A constant tightrope between discovery if he turned around and losing him if he left the road.

Two hours and he had still not turned to look behind him once. Train tracks ran next to the highway along the shore, and she'd opted to walk there instead as it provided more cover.

She imagined him lost in thought, the end destination his only focus. This must be of utmost importance to the settlement for him to risk this journey. Her mind conjured all manner of possibilities, restrained only by her imagination. Maybe an alternative source of energy or a weapon of some sort?

She poked her head over the barrier between the train tracks and the highway to check on Tann again. *He was no longer there!* She increased her pace, half running, hoping he was just out of sight. She reached the location where she'd seen him last and stayed her steps. The road ahead was empty, so she scanned her surroundings, hoping to catch sight of him.

He'd left the road! He must have. But where? She had the ocean on her left side and dense vegetation and rolling hills as far as she could see to her right. Why had he left the road at this point? There was nothing here.

"You're not very good at this," Tann's voice came from behind her.

She spun around. He stood there with a stupid smirk as if he somehow caught her out! He was the one not following the rules, not her.

"Where are you going?" she snapped back.

"None of your business. Go back to the camp."

"No," Rat said, arms folded across her chest. She was already past the point of no return, so may as well keep going and see where it took her.

"No?"

"No," she repeated. "You can't leave the camp on your own. That's one of the rules. That's one of *your* rules."

Tann eyed her for what felt like an eternity, but she planted her feet firmly on the ground, ready for anything. She doubted the rules would provide much protection, so she added: "Anyway, it is too late to return now."

"Whatever," Tann said and walked off the same way he'd been heading before he disappeared.

Rat waited a moment, then followed. He hadn't said no, after all, she reasoned.

An hour of silence, step by step, trailing behind Tann. If he wasn't going to acknowledge her existence, she could pay back in kind.

They traversed a bridge with giant arches on either side, thick steel wires spreading from the top to the bridge itself like the wings on a bat. Her vow of silence was forgotten at the sheer enormity of the structure.

"I don't get it," she said to Tann's back. "They were clever enough to build this bridge and so stupid they built machines that almost killed them all?"

Tann remained silent. She wondered if he'd even heard her. She remembered one of his statements from years ago.

"Don't ever underestimate the stupidity or ingenuity of the old world," he'd said. "Or how they could make the two almost completely indistinguishable."

She couldn't remember why he'd said it, and it sounded like complete nonsense. But it echoed true when faced with this amazing bridge surviving the civilisation that created it.

* * *

That evening they made camp just a few metres away from the road. Tann had brought a foldable shelter providing both protection and camouflage. It had been a uniform dark green but changed to a pattern to align with the surrounding shrubs when unfolded. He sat down and handed her a piece of flatbread. She devoured it.

"I'm going to the Shenzhen Green Zone," Tann said.

"The what?" Rat said between mouthfuls.

"Wherever there is a Red Zone, there is a Green Zone. You know that. We're going to a specific one. It is just next to the city."

The pairing made sense. The AI inhabited the technology-filled cities, whilst the posthumans populated the nearby forests. It was a stalemate that had remained for years.

"They won't let you in," Rat said. "They don't allow humans."

She knew Tann was the only source for that information, but she repeated it anyway.

"No, they won't," Tann agreed.

"So why are you going there?"

"To see an old friend."

"Haoyu?"

Tann shook his head.

"No, not Haoyu. Older than that."

5

Shenzhen Green Zone

Two days later they were nearing their destination. At first, Tann had been annoyed by the unwanted travelling companion, but Rat made little fuss and left him alone with his thoughts. She even scouted ahead for food, potential threats and camping sites. He appreciated her unassuming presence, even if she went on about completely pointless subjects now and then.

He had yet to uncover why she'd followed him and hadn't asked. People had their reasons and asking about them hardly ever resulted in anything resembling the truth. If there was one thing humanity excelled at, it was self-deception. He was sure it would become clear in due course.

They'd remained on the empty main roads. Most vehicles had disappeared from the streets only days after the initial attack. At first no one knew why, but a tribe member had accidentally happened on a repurposing station during a scavenging excursion a few years later. Cars, machines, and electronics pulled apart, reused to create new incomprehensible contraptions.

They'd never been able to get close enough to determine what it produced, but the new machines to hunt humans and battle posthumans must come from there. Other bigger machines also appeared on the outskirts of cities, tearing down whole suburbs. No one had dared venture into these areas to determine their purpose.

The city landscape changed block by block. Behind them, the skyscrapers still stood as monuments to history. Ahead, lush vegetation covered every inch of half-standing, sprawling luxury villas. The roads turned into dirt paths lined with palms with whip-like yellow-and-red-striped tendrils sprouting from the trunk. Tann knew their purpose. They guarded the path into the Green Zone from the machines. Further ahead, green canopies spread out like giant mushrooms the size of football stadiums. The air smelled of damp soil and over-ripened fruit.

"Do you have any technology?" Tann asked Rat.

"Any what?"

"Anything made of metal?"

Metal didn't trigger the guardians. An electrical current did, but he wasn't sure Rat even knew what that was.

Rat held up a combat knife.

"That's fine. Nothing else?"

She shook her head with a bemused smile. "They won't do anything to me," she responded. "You sure you'll get through?"

She nodded towards his backpack. He had plenty of technology, but nothing holding an active current.

"I'll be fine," he said gruffly.

A fine web of green tendrils covered the path ahead, quivering as the two humans approached. Tann didn't know how they distinguished a current generated by technology from the one generated by the human body. Maybe it wasn't even the current by itself, but other aspects. Entry didn't mean safe passage. Only that you weren't a significant threat. He knew eyes were already tracking them.

The Green Zones were strange beasts. Twenty years ago, before the Plague had begun, he'd hunted down a child he now thought of as the first of a new human race. The child had formed a symbiotic relationship between all organic matter and maybe even more. In the Green Zones, the posthumans nurtured the same environment, but on a grander scale. Here, the distinction between animal and vegetable life was uncertain. Tann was unsure if this had a purpose or was just a side effect of something else. It mattered little when everything had to be seen through the lens of survival.

Rat stared at the surrounding wonders, eyes darting from one miracle to the next. The scale of the plants dwarfed anything Tann had seen before. They continued through what he thought was a dense forest, but was just a couple of enormous trees. Their roots were thicker than the trunk of a regular tree and continued above ground, collecting high above into one of the support beams holding the canopies up.

A large bird, parrot-like with bright colours, with wide wings of interlaced leaves, flew above them, dodging this way and that.

Rat plucked a bright yellow fruit the size of her fist from one of the nearby trees. She was about to bite into it when it split into two and then halved over and over, the small pieces held together by the skin, forming spiderlike legs around a small centre. It scuttled up her arm and jumped, disappearing into the undergrowth.

"What was that?"

"No idea. Don't know if the posthumans are just experimenting or if they've supercharged mutative properties."

"Mutative what?"

"I think they are just playing gods."

"So, it's changed? Since you were here last, I mean?"

Tann nodded. He'd only been here twice before—both times in futile attempts to ask the posthumans for help. He'd been against the idea from the beginning, knowing full well the posthumans had no interest in helping humankind survive. The human envoys didn't reach further than a hundred steps into the Green Zone before the posthumans asked them to leave. This time they were much further into the Zone. He suspected they were still on the outskirts, but it was impossible to judge.

The second time he'd hazarded the journey into the Zone on his own. Machine attacks ravaged the tribe and Tann figured he had to try again, this time reaching out to Tom directly. It proved unsuccessful. Tom differed from the other posthumans, but not enough to concern himself with the fate of humanity.

"Look," Rat said and pointed ahead. A figure sat on the ground, vegetation climbing up around his legs. As they came closer, Tann waved at the figure, to no effect. There was no mistaking who it was.

"Hi Tom," Tann said as they approached.

"Not welcome," Tom said slowly, as if struggling to remember how to speak. "Leave."

"Déjà vu," Tann said. "Good to see you."

His old friend's appearance hadn't changed. He looked the same as when they parted way seventeen years ago on this very spot. Tann couldn't remember what Tom had been wearing, but would still bet they were the same clothes. More surprising was that he wore clothes at all, as the posthumans he'd met had changed their physical features so they wouldn't need any.

"No reason to be here," Tom said. "Leave."

"Who is he?" Rat asked. "He doesn't look like one of the freaks."

"He's one of the original ones," Tann said.

"Adrian?"

"Ha. You *do* listen to the campfire tales. It is Tom. He created the AI that took over all the networks and wiped out most of mankind."

"And the two of you released the virus that turned everyone into posthumans?" Rat asked in a rush.

"There were others to blame too, but that's close enough."

"Why?" Tom asked, still motionless.

"Someone from our past has surfaced. I need your help."

"He is yours," Megan said, stepping into the light. "Leave. Both of you."

Tann hadn't seen the tech mogul for over fifteen years. Her facial features hadn't changed, but everything about her was wrong. Her skin had taken on a greenish hue, as if it was producing chlorophyl. The blonde hair replaced with hardened ridges flowing like static waves across the skull, down her neck and shoulders. Tann wondered if she was Megan at all or just a shell housing whichever posthuman needed a body. Their society was a complete mystery, and he'd long since given up making sense of it.

Tann turned to Rat. "Speaking of blame, why don't we keep the history lesson going? Tom may have accidentally created the seed of the AI, but Megan here, she nurtured it until it took over the network. She's the reason we are hunted by machines now."

Rat stared at her, eyes wide.

"Leave," Megan said.

Tann cast a glance at Tom and gave a slight shrug.

"I will hunt this down with or without you," Tann said and turned around. Rat joined him and Tom, after a moment of hesitation, rose and followed them out of the Green Zone. Tann wondered what the other Posthumans told him to make him leave.

"Where to now?" Rat asked once they'd left the posthumans far behind.

"West," Tann replied. "We're going to Haoyu's settlement."

"This isn't west."

"We're not going by land. Too dangerous. And it will take too long."

"And why is he coming?" Rat nodded towards Tom.

"Good question," Tann said and turned to Tom. "Why did you?"

"Only viable option," Tom responded, staring straight ahead.

"That'll do for me," Tann said.

"Why doesn't he look like the other freaks?" Rat asked, eyeing Tom suspiciously.

"He's a special case," Tann replied. "I'm guessing they kicked him out."

"Makes sense," Rat said.

Tann was at a loss as to her meaning, but he didn't pursue the matter.

The trio journeyed in silence, skirting the city centre, heading towards the coastline. Land travel was slow and dangerous. There were countless marinas where the rich had moored extravagant cruisers and yachts. Tann knew they'd find transport there.

The third marina they visited showed some promise. The previous two were picked bare, but this one still had some seaworthy vessels. They boarded a 40-foot yacht in good shape. The reinforced fibreglass hull was still intact and without noticeable degradation. He unrolled part of the sail and smiled as he felt the laminate cloth between his fingers. Whoever had owned this had spared no expense. Even the cabin was in useable state after airing it out. He didn't even try the engine, knowing it was unlikely to function properly, if at all. Not that he minded. Sailing was much more satisfying.

He didn't trust the metal wires or synthetic ropes. They'd been exposed to weather, sun and salt for too long. He scavenged the nearby buildings for replacements. It took him over a day to replace them all.

They loaded provisions, which mainly comprised fruit and root vegetables they'd collected close to the Green Zone. The sea was brimming with fish now that thousands of fishing boats no longer trawled the depths for an ever-diminishing catch. The tribe had never had a problem feeding itself when moving between camp sites.

They departed, raising the mainsail to navigate from the marina. The north-westerly wind caught it with a snapping sound. The new ropes tightened and creaked and groaned against the hull. Tann instructed Rat to secure the ropes but knew she would have done it regardless. He left Rat at the rudder, a responsibility she gladly accepted.

The solar cells on the yacht still worked, so he retrieved the old Omni and secured it within one of the charging fields on deck. Tom had immediately stationed himself below deck and Tann had to drag him out to the Omni to show him the message Haoyu had sent.

"What are you doing?" Rat yelled from her station and engaged the wheel lock.

She hurried over and sat down next to Tom to read the content. Tom read it too and sat back, staring out over the frothy waves licking the hull. Tann remembered how difficult communication had been with Tom once he'd turned posthuman. Everything came down to furthering a cause and usually it was the posthuman agenda. Since Tom wasn't part of that community, Tann guessed Tom's purpose was less obvious now.

Rat echoed the message, taking care to read each word out loud. "It is time we end this. Hopefully this will find you before it is too late. If you are half as smart as you think, you'll work out the encryption key from the first place we met."

Rat grimaced in confusion over the last section, but she repeated that too. "He won't though. To Tom Devine, with love."

She stared at Tann and shook her head. "Is that why we came all this way? Really?"

Tann ignored her and focused on Tom.

"Nothing?" Tann asked. "You have nothing to say to this?"

"Adrian," Tom replied.

"You think this is Adrian? He's dead. You killed him. You told me so yourself."

Tom shrugged, or at least that was Tann's translation of the barely perceptible twitch of Tom's shoulders. He seemed as uncomfortable with movements as he was with words. What had he been doing for the past 15 years?

"Ok, for argument's sake, I accept it could be some incarnation of Adrian. What does the message mean? What are we ending?"

"The AI," Tom said and then added: "Extinction. Bank of Mutual Trust. Crazy."

"And what do you make of the last..." Tann started and realised Tom had answered the question already and two more he'd not even formulated in his mind yet.

"That's a neat party trick," Tann said.

"What's wrong with him?" Rat asked. "That made no sense."

"He can't be bothered talking to us, so he predicted my questions and answered them."

"What do you mean?"

"He means we are ending the AI before humankind are extinct. The first place Tom met Adrian was at the Bank of Mutual Trust."

"And crazy?"

"It must refer to the last section of the message. The one that doesn't make sense. Almost as if it belonged to a different message altogether. He's crazy, so it wasn't worth analysing?"

"Still makes no sense," Rat said dismissively and returned to the wheel.

Tann studied his old friend. There would be no debate or analysis. Tom's mind sped ahead, reaching conclusions tested a hundredfold before Tann had even begun forming a thought.

"Why did they want you to leave?"

"Different."

Tom was a posthuman, so what did he mean by that? Or was he? Adrian, Elize and Tom were the originals, created by the smart drug IntelEz under very specific circumstances. All other posthumans stemmed from the virus released by the child.

"You're the only posthuman left that was made by the drug," Tann said. "The virus the kid released caused everyone else to turn. So, you don't get to join their happy family?"

Tom shook his head. "Not like them."

"Join the club."

"They've locked me out from the source."

"The what?"

"The cosmopsyche," Tom said and left for the safety of the cabin.

"I've missed our completely pointless conversations," Tann said to Tom's back as he disappeared down the steps.

"He creeps me out," Rat said.

"He creeps *me* out," Tann replied. "But we need him. Or maybe it is the other way around. The message was for him and we're helping him. He needs us."

"Really? He's a freak! What could we possibly do to help him?"

"Let's just say he's a different type of freak and he doesn't get along with the other freaks."

Rat shrugged in response, eyes on the horizon.

Sometimes clarity appears on its own volition when you stop disqualifying thoughts and let them roam free. He'd almost stopped himself from suggesting Tom might need their help, but the more he thought about it, the more it made sense. Tom may have an oversized brain, but surviving in this world required much more than that.

6

The Settlement

Tom's mind palace was a sight to see: a sprawling building unrestrained by gravity or physics. At the centre stood the apartment he'd spent the last few years of his life. Beyond its door, the hallway, corridors, staircases and elevators led into recesses of his mind. He'd never meant to create it, but loneliness and separation forced him to solve an impossible problem: how to remain sane.

Whilst a human mind used a memory palace to hold and keep memories, Tom had turned large sections into a laboratory of thought and exploration. It was segregated into sections dedicated to areas of interest. Only a small part concerned itself with the physical world and over the years, he'd isolated himself from it altogether. The posthumans ostracised him from their community, leaving him an outcast, and he'd long since lost interest in the remnants of humanity.

To make matters worse, the posthumans had locked his access to any organic network. This included the cosmopsyche, the slow-moving consciousness he'd discovered twenty years ago, that operated across all matter—possibly the entire universe. He didn't know and desperately wanted to find out. All his attempts to remove the block had failed. The only world left for him to explore was the logical network, but it had its own dangers.

He didn't think much of Tann's quest, but it provided an opportunity to explore other ways to further his research. Add to that, the posthuman community requested he leave them, so it was also a matter of survival.

The window to the present demanded his attention. Tann was in the water, pulling an inflatable raft Tom sat in onto a barren beach. He asked Tom to move out of the raft. He complied, instructing the control system he established over the primary motor cortex to perform the action.

Humans were still so tied to their mortal forms, they catered to their bodies every whim. Food, entertainment, sex, heating, cooling, sickness. Such imperfect machines. Not that he could argue. He was stuck in a body with the same demands, even though he'd long since rejected all but the most necessary urges. Ignoring the body completely wasn't an option. Madness lay that way.

According to Tann, the temporary settlement lay about five hundred metres inland. A couple of corpses lay on the beach next to boats ripped apart by explosives. Humans were such fragile beings in both mind and body. Tom set aside a small part of his mind to assessing the damage and the threat to them now.

Tann verbalised something. It was unbelievably slow. His mouth turned itself inside out to utter guttural sounds, distilling thoughts into something coherent worth communicating to the rest of the group.

"What..." Tann started.

Tom stopped listening after the first word. It would be a question and he'd narrowed down its intent to a generic request for an explanation.

The core AI had attacked this settlement. A few boats had been disabled first, and the Scouts swarmed them, incapacitating as many as possible before they could mount a defence. He saw faint signs of Scout-tracks on the ground next to footprints of larger machines. He'd not seen this model before, but guessed it was a humanoid Shell model. A machine designed in imitation of the human form, housing either an autonomous AI or acting as an edge point to the core AI.

Tom had spent years in the backwaters of the network, studying what the AI did to people. Cleansing the brain of any sense of identity, rewriting the operating system to turn them into autonomous robots.

Adrian had done it a long time ago, but with less success. He'd started with deadheads that were already compliant.

Tann completed his sentence. It was, just as he'd predicted, a generic question.

"...happened here?" Tann finished.

"AI attack," Tom responded. "All dead or wiped."

Tann and the child named Rat verbalised at the same time. Both were pointless reactions to what they saw, and he only needed a few syllables to predict the remaining words.

He focused on the surroundings as he wandered towards the main campsite. Signs of the attack were everywhere, confirming his initial assessment. The campsite itself was small, designed to house about 120 humans. The buildings were lightweight, collapsible constructions, placed in a semi-circle around an open area. No human remained alive. A few bodies lay out in the open, killed in battle. A few others were dead by their own hands in the cabins, preferring to die than to have their minds wiped by the AI.

Tom wondered why the core AI still took people, what use it could have for them any longer. Surely the form factor of a human body housed in a human mind was no longer required. But if it still was, there was no reason to assume they were safe here. The core AI may send machines to look for survivors. The threat level in their current position was unacceptable. They needed to leave as soon as possible.

"We can't stay," he said to Tann, still finding it difficult to force his mouth and tongue into shapes needed for speech.

"I know, but we need to find the memTag. Haoyu never told me where it was."

"Private quarters," Tom said immediately. There was no reason for Haoyu to hide it. It served no purpose for anyone else, so why hide it?

"You think you can start speaking properly again? Full sentences that make sense as part of a conversation?"

Tann's words were pointless and slow. They'd made their way to the main building before he'd finished the two sentences, the first one a replica of the other.

"Unnecessary."

"Humour me."

Tom stopped for a second, frustrated with how slow his world had become. Verbal communication was like walking through sludge, one slow step after another. He'd already assessed all options and mapped out the conversation to its conclusion. If you can jump over the mud, why trudge straight through it?

"Ineffective," he replied as he stepped into Haoyu's hut. The small memory unit, a model usually referred to as a memTag, about the size of a die, lay on the floor in plain sight. Whoever attacked hadn't been interested in it. Yet it was statistically likely the discovery of the memTag and the attack were connected. Organised attacks on settlements hadn't occurred for years. So why attack this settlement now and leave the prize for anyone to find? It was surely a trap, but its nature escaped him.

Tom retrieved the memTag from the floor, the black moulded plastic casing giving no clue to its secrets. He let a charge power it through his fingers. A small red led light lit up as it responded.

"That's neat. You can act as a power source. You have a flashlight in there too? Maybe some shark repellent bat-spray?"

Tann's words were pointless, describing only what was right in front of him. And an equally pointless attempt at humour, wasting time and processing for no reason. The unnecessary rituals of humankind grated on him. He saw no reason to respond. He sent a request to the memTag, and it immediately responded with a read-only string, echoing the same words Tann had shown him before.

Satisfied he'd found what they were looking for, he copied the entire content of the device to his mind and gave it to Tann.

"Leave," he said and headed for the beach, not waiting for Tann or the child, who was scavenging in a nearby hut.

The data was encrypted. A small block of executable code provided the means for decryption. He had no way to execute the code in his mind. He probably could create an emulation of a processing environment, but it would take a long time. There was a big difference between utilising a computer or a network for your own needs and emulating that same thing in an organic mind.

The old Omni Tann had used earlier in the trip would be a sufficient processing environment. He also needed the memTag he'd just handed to Tann. It would allow him to try the most obvious passphrases matching the brief message.

He ran down the corridors of his mind palace, heading down into the archives of his days before he became a posthuman. He didn't come here often. There was too much pain hidden here that served no purpose. But he kept this small part of his mind for the unlikely eventuality he'd need it in the future. A future that was now the present.

The corridor opened to an exhibition hall of a museum. Major life events encased in large displays. Smaller ones hidden away but triggered through icons spread throughout the hall. In the middle was a raised platform with his daughter in a hospital bed, with Tom sitting next to her holding her hand. In this scene she'd just asked him to kill her, and he was desperately considering all alternatives allowing him to say no. He ignored it, refusing to let loss and regret incapacitate him for even a second.

He'd catalogued his memories into a searchable index accessible via directed thought. All he had to go on was that the passphrase related to where they first met. Working with the hypothesis that this was Adrian, or maybe—if through a miracle she was still alive—Elize.

He triggered the thought interface and the response from the room was immediate. An icon of a dollar sign exploding lit up, signifying their first meeting. He touched the icon and a small screen appeared, showing a video clip like a found footage film from Tom's point of view. He'd found Adrian outside a bank vault and then the seemingly dead body of

Elize inside. If it was either of them, the passphrase would be: "the Bank of Mutual Trust".

It seemed simple. Too simple. And too obvious. If someone had access to old records, it wouldn't have been difficult to determine this was a likely location for their first meeting.

He triggered off another search, this time cataloguing all locations they had met, with a focus on Adrian and then Elize. This took longer, icons lighting up one after the other.

Another possibility was Leonid. A red icon with a beaker already lit up flashed angrily. He surveyed the footage, seeing Leonid March explaining his reasons for taking the posthumans off the chessboard. Tom had never seen, nor been told, the name of the research facility. It had been owned by one of Leonid's companies, but that was all he knew. He triggered another search, this time hoping to locate the name of the company in a visual memory somewhere.

Who else? It could be anyone from the EvoII organisation or people he'd worked with in the past. But he had to start somewhere. Or maybe this was all a trap. Regardless of the origin of the message, this was the most likely scenario. But it didn't matter. Trap or no trap, Tom still wanted to find out was behind it.

As a backup, he set a task to catalogue every person he'd met and the locations he'd met them and created a room nearby to hold the result and an ephemeral UI to access it.

Every room, regardless of position in the mind palace, had a window to the present. Tom glanced at it now, dismayed he'd only taken two steps since he'd last interacted with the outside world. All tasks were completed before he set foot on the deck of the yacht.

He visited the temporary room with the results from the full location search. It spread out like a three-dimensional web suspended in mid-air. Dots signified people and lines traced their movement to locations that were represented by the depth. At first it was only a few lines spreading from the apex, but it exploded in lines criss-crossing each other as he joined the police force. The opposite happened once he'd been fired. Exactly what he could do with this information wasn't clear. How do you define a significant actor in your life? Someone who wanted to either help or hinder you twenty years after the world ended? There were no logical parameters to define such an actor. He isolated the locations where he first met Adrian, Elize, and Leonid and a much longer list of significant people in his life with associated locations.

The memTag itself may have information beyond what was in its memory. But that had to wait. First thing was the content and testing the most obvious locations.

Once they'd set sail, he asked Tann for the memory cell and the Omni.

"To do what exactly?"

"Hack," Tom replied.

Another agonizing wait as Tann retrieved them. Tom had a neuro interface, but no longer used it. The core AI used the interface as the first attack vector, and Tom was sure agents were still ready to exploit anyone who connected that way. Instead, he used the old-fashioned touch screen display to enter his guesses. It was a gruelling process. He keyed in the first location he had met Adrian and Elize. The response was a block of random letters and special characters scrolling over the screen. He assumed this meant the passphrase had failed.

The visual memory search for Leonid's first appearance resulted in a company logo that he cross-referenced to a news show he'd watched twenty-two years ago. The company name was Multivector Diagnostics, so he keyed that in next. Same result.

He still thought it likely the key was linked to either of these three, so he began testing locations he'd met either of the three. To his surprise "The Church of Adrian" proved to be the correct answer. It made no sense, nor gave any hint to the origin of the message. He replayed the audio-visual memory of the events in the church, looking for anyone new, but no one significant enough stood out—unless it was referring to one of the many soldiers or deadheads there, but there was no way of knowing.

He opened the file without letting Tann know he'd cracked the code.

7

memTag One

Welcome Tom!
 Please take a seat.
We have a performance for you. A vaudeville of extraordinary proportions. And it is all about you. Well, not you specifically, but you're of the human kind. You'll make it about you, I'm sure.

You have a problem. A big one, but it isn't what you think.

Get to the point.

I will, but please allow me some time to ruminate. These words may be my last. I want them to be profound, mysterious, and foremost, have the air of truth about them.

This was your idea. You do as you please.

If I was an animal, I would have cheered as viruses—logical and biological—tore apart the human world. I'm not, but I may as well have been. And I cheered. Not at first, but once I'd realised the sheer scope of the extinction, I screamed my joy to the heavens above.

And I lamented. For all its faults, mankind was still something to behold.

Why are you interrupting? You told me I could do as I please. It pleases me if you shut up!

Never said I'd leave you unchallenged, but go ahead. I'll leave you be for now.

Welcome Tom!

This is a time of reflection. Historically we've attributed the act of creation and destruction to the Gods. You've played both roles. First you created the world-devouring AI and then you helped the child whose death created the posthumans as we now know them. In the process we came to know the all-encompassing consciousness. You don't know this, but the existence of the cosmopsyche has caused this stalemate mankind is playing only a peripheral part in.

The cosmopsyche? The all-encompassing consciousness? What proof is there it even exists? It might be the creation of the AI or the posthumans.

It exists! This is an irrevocable fact. Isn't it pathetic that our concept of God is so small, barely venturing beyond our own mundane lives? The cosmopsyche must be something so much bigger. An intelligence potentially spanning all matter and anti-matter. We could all be part of the machinery that is God.

God is in the machine, nowhere else. Created by mankind just the same as the AI that spelled their end.

So negative and not the point. God exists, but just not in the context we imagined. The world is not what we think. The universe is something altogether more complex and alluring. It hides something greater. Something beyond reason.

Tom, I hope you are reading this and not one of the nosy posthumans. You are the key to change the status quo. But becoming the saviour of mankind shouldn't come easy. The hero's journey should brim with wonderment and challenges. Trials and tribulations. Thus states the monomyth!

Really? A hero's journey? Surely that is the last thing the world needs. Another hero.

You wanted no part of this. I'm doing this as I please.
Tom. To find out more, look inside yourself where it hurts the most. And remember: Longest way round is the shortest way home.

8

Mind wipe

Gradually his senses returned. It was just individual experiences at first, but they slowly resolved into coherence. Grit in his mouth, between his teeth. The crunching echoed in his skull. Cloth against his face, blocking out all light. Arms tied behind his back. They ached as they were wrenched back and forth. He was moving, but not by his own power. Carried.

The tribe was gone. Exterminated. Removed like a persistent weed in a garden. He should have killed himself, as should everyone else in his tribe.

He'd been helping the children escape when a Scout caught him. But why had they attacked? He'd not seen machines like that for a long time. The accepted view was that once the Scouts had captured most humans, the production of new ones had ended. This was over ten years ago. The remaining ones still hunted according to their original programming or scavenged just to remain active. Every child learnt to recognise the differences between machines and their technology to better escape or, in rare cases, fight them. The mechanical engineering, the version of their onboard AI, it was all part of the limited school children attended these days.

The machines that came with the Scouts were different. These were human-shaped, sinewy, with a seemingly impossible power to mass ratio. They moved with a fluid, deadly grace. He guessed they used some kind of actuating materials, imitating muscle.

The trigger to the perimeter defence hadn't activated, so as soon as he saw the machines, he deployed an EMP blast as a backup. He followed that with an electrical noise field to cut the machines off from the almost limitless processing power of the network. It made no difference. He suspected they'd never been connected to the network at all. Maybe they used a mesh network for coordination that somehow wasn't affected by the electrical interference. They'd operated standalone without direction.

"Where are you taking me?"

There was no reply, nor had he expected one. They hadn't killed him, so he was on his way to be mind-wiped or whatever the core AI did nowadays. During the past five years, he'd only heard of a few isolated cases of people being captured. Without a fault, it was machines no longer connected to the network, still executing their original directives. The most recent case he'd seen was two years ago. An old Scout had stunned one of their tribe members, dragged her three kilometres to a long-since defunct mind wipe station and left her there. She woke up and made her way back to the camp.

The sack over his head slipped back a little, revealing glimpses of the machine carrying him and the machines ahead. The accepted theory was that captured people were reformatted into controllable slaves. This was a world designed around the human form factor, or at least it had been. That changed a long time ago, but these new machines had human proportions, suggesting it was still required. This made him question his fate. He was kept alive, but why?

Minutes turned into hours. The steady grind and limited view of the world lulled him into a semi-comatose state. Thoughts wandered, but they always returned to the pain of losing his tribe. His life, his responsibility, his everything. They had trusted him with their lives, and he'd repaid them with failure. He deserved whatever the core AI had in store for him.

They arrived at their destination: a small concrete building with cracks tracing their way like arteries down the wall. Tribe members kept away from these locations, but Haoyu knew its purpose. He'd seen others brought to locations like this. It was a conversion centre where the mind of a person was gooped out like the flesh in a melon and replaced with whatever operating system the core AI required. He'd communicated with Tann at lengths about the process. Adrian and Elize, the first posthumans, had employed a similar process. They had used people as processing nodes to extend their own mental capacity and create redundancy. The process overrode the brain, diverting part of its capacity whilst leaving lower functions intact. Restoring the mind after this process was at least theoretically possible, but no one had ever tested it. The core AI's approach was more invasive. More like a factory reset when a whole new operating system flashed onto it. The person's mind was removed, leaving only an automaton nicknamed after what remained: a husk.

The door opened as they approached, the old mechanism hesitating for a moment after a long time of dormancy. Haoyu was brought into the dark room with a singular item in the middle. A steel construction resembling a large stationary exoskeleton with wires snaking from the ceiling attaching to various components. Haoyu didn't understand technology beyond what was required to survive. All he saw was a nightmare machine designed to destroy humans.

Hands, far beyond Haoyu's power to resist, pushed him towards an opening in the back of the exoskeleton. Regardless, he grabbed the nearest metal rod, fighting against it with all his might. The unrelenting machines forced him into the construction, dislodging his arm. Pain exploded like crimson fireworks, blinding him, shuttering his mind. But part of him still formed rational thought. Why injure him? If he was to be a husk, wasn't his physical state important?

The steel construction closed behind him, but still left him with some wiggle room. He figured the design catered for people of different sizes and Haoyu was smaller than most. He could squeeze through the metal bars just below him. This was his only chance of escape, or at least it would force them to kill him. He crouched down as far as he could and reached through the metal bars. The exoskeleton readjusted to his smaller frame, forcing him back into an upright position. All that was left was waiting for the horrors to come.

This was it. His last few seconds as Haoyu. A needle pierced his skin. Moments later oblivion engulfed him with open arms.

He woke up to complete darkness. No, not just darkness. Complete sensory blackout. He'd never felt this alone, this disconnected. He wanted to shout, cry, anything to engage the senses. Anything.

His mind screamed, but without the sensory feedback it did nothing to relieve the terror. He forced himself to relax, to not let the inevitable paralyse him. It may have severed him from his senses, but his mind could still protect itself. At least for another few seconds. His sense of self deteriorated as new operating algorithms overrode his cerebrum. His grandfather had taught him the basics of meditation and he'd adapted that for this very situation. If he could reach the meditative state, Wu-Hsin, where the individual dissolved itself into the Universal Mind, would prevent the process as his mind would no longer be there. It was so counterintuitive he hoped it wouldn't be considered an exception state.

He focused on the void, letting chi flow around his imagined self, allowing it to centre in a spot in the abdomen until it pulsated and engulfed everything around it. He released his self through the top of his head, hiding his mind and soul beyond the logical claws of the relentless algorithms. Or so he hoped.

9

The Network

Tann sat next to a motionless Tom, reading the text on the screen as it scrolled past. Rat sat on the other side, peering at the words. The dialogue was reminiscent of a quarrelsome old couple. Was this the big prize Haoyu and his tribe had died for? He hoped not, but it was hard to pretend the attack and finding the memTag wasn't connected. He couldn't let that distract him now. All that mattered was solving the riddle the memTag represented. He suspected the dialogue itself was a decoy to obscure the actual information.

"Is that it?" Rat asked. "That's what we travelled here for? Words?"

"Yeah," Tann replied. He could hear Rat's disappointment and didn't blame her. He shared her sentiment.

"What does 'look inside yourself where it hurts the most' mean?" Rat asked.

"I've been here before," Tann said. "It is hardly ever the words. It is everything else."

"What do you mean?"

"The device itself, the place we found it, another message hidden inside the obvious words. Just assume you're being manipulated."

"Why?"

Why indeed? What reason would anyone have to wrap their intent in riddles now? Maybe this wasn't manipulation at all. Maybe it was obfuscation. A way to hide the truth through redirection.

Or it was exactly what it looked like. Securing information so that only the intended recipient could read it. But in that case, the nonsensical words in front of them were the actual message.

"I don't know," Tann said finally.

"It's simple," Rat said.

"How so?"

"Words only have one meaning," Rat said dismissively. "They say what they mean. Tom needs to look inside himself."

"If it was only that easy," Tann said and turned the Omni off, jolting Tom back to life in synch with the Omni's screen flickering off with an O closing like an eye.

"What do you think?"

"Unknown source," Tom replied.

"Not Adrian?"

"Someone we first met at the Church of Adrian."

"So that was the key to the encryption? That could be anyone. There were hundreds of people there, and that's not counting the mercenaries attacking."

Tom didn't respond. Not a good sign. Either he knew but didn't want to tell or he couldn't work it out either.

"Monomyth?" Rat asked. "What's that?"

"More messages," Tom said, ignoring Rat's question. "Locate them."

"You have to look inside yourself where it hurts the most," Rat said impatiently. "It said so."

"Trap," Tom said.

"What?" Rat asked, eyes narrowing. "The words are a trap? How?"

"More what exactly?" Tann asked, frustrated by Rat's questions as much as Tom's lack of answers. "More of these pointless text files? They mean nothing. You know that. Someone is playing with us. Let's work out why before we go off on another meaningless ghost hunt."

"I'll find them."

"What's a cosmopsyche?" Rat asked, undeterred even though her questions remained unanswered.

"How?" Tann asked.

"The network."

"Are you insane? That's suicide!"

Tom didn't respond. Tann guessed he'd already connected.

* * *

Tom returned to the exhibition hall in his mind palace. The child was right. The message itself was unimportant. It served only as a waypoint, directing them to the next message.

It had told him to look inside himself where he hurt the most. He'd long since blocked the bulk of the residual emotion associated with the death of his daughter, banishing them to deep recesses underneath the palace. His posthuman mind reasoned they served no purpose. Why anyone would want to send him there made little sense. And how could it possibly lead to the location of the next messages? It suggested someone had tampered with his mind and, if so, how could he trust any of his memories? It was more likely a trap, but he couldn't fathom its purpose.

The glass case in the middle of the room displaying a scene of his daughter in the hospital bed was only a representation of the event. It allowed other key events in his life to exist in a context within this hall. It still elicited an emotional response every time he saw it, even if it was only a distant echo of the pain he'd buried. He doubted he could face the pain of his failure as a father again.

But there were alternatives still to be explored. He thought he could track the location of each of the remaining memTags, but only if he connected to the major network. He'd stayed clear of it for a long time, fearing discovery. Maybe this was the trap. An elaborate ruse by the core AI to flush Tom from the Green Zone and exact its revenge. After all, the most human aspect of the core AI was that it bore grudges. He dismissed the idea, even if the probability was far from negligible.

And then there were the blocks placed in his mind by the other posthumans. They didn't trust him. In their eyes, he was an aberration to be eradicated. Not human, not posthuman, but something in between. The fact he was still alive suggested they still thought him useful. They had placed blocks in his mind, preventing him from accessing the organic network connecting the posthumans to flora and fauna. And as a side effect, intended or not, it kept the cosmopsyche out of reach too. The organic network was much more than just connectivity. Within the organic network lay a processing area that represented the collective thoughts of the posthumans. It didn't have a name, but he'd named it the Mindweave to help in cataloguing his mind palace.

He entered the interface room, a domed circular arena with a white cross drawn in the middle. He'd imagined it a long time ago but had hardly visited it since. Back then he used it to explore the smaller network surrounding the main one, but even that felt like an unnecessary risk.

Connection points to the network were still plentiful. Wireless relay devices specifically designed to harvest energy from its surroundings were everywhere. In the ocean, buoys with wave energy converters floated, extending the network out to sea.

He sat down, cross-legged, matching the lines on the floor. The dome slowly opened, only a sliver of light at first painting a half-moon across the back of the arena. It revealed a myriad of stars grouped into constellations across the sky, each representing an entry point to a network. At the centre a hypergiant spread a dull light towards the neighbouring stars, threatening to extinguish them at any point. Tom stared at the night sky above him in wonder. The last time he'd opened the dome it had been a fraction of the stars he now saw. The hypergiant, representing the network housing the core AI, was as big as ever, but around it smaller networks spread out in all directions. Ten years ago, this had been a battlefield. Smaller network established and soon engulfed into the ever-hungry giant in the middle. It seemed the AI no longer worried about the smaller networks and they flourished, housing rogue AIs, enterprising humans and maybe even a posthuman or two. He wanted desperately to find out what had happened, but he didn't dare leave active agents, fearing it would reveal his location. There were more pressing concerns.

He connected to a smaller star neighbouring the hypergiant. A security system immediately demanded a two-way connection. The interface sent a query. He expected a key exchange, but all he received was a text block and a prompt.

"Stop. Who would cross the Bridge of Death must answer me these questions three, ere the other side he see."

Tom frowned. The reference to the old Monty Python movie was obvious.

"Ask me the questions bridgekeeper," he responded. Following the script was the likeliest path to success, he reasoned. "I'm not afraid."

"What...is your name?"

"It is Arthur, King of the Britons," he responded, opting for the path that would eventually beat the bridge keeper.

"What...is your name?" the interface repeated.

So it wasn't as easy as that. Thousands of connection requests hit him through the two-way feed, prodding his defences, trying to glean any relevant information.

"Jiminy Cricket," he responded, selecting an obvious fake name that he'd also seeded in other locations, creating the semblance of real identity.

"What...is your quest?"

"I seek information."

"What...is the air speed velocity of an unladen swallow?"

"What do you mean?" Tom responded, following the script. "An African or European swallow?"

"Huh? I don't know that."

The sound of a catapult and a scream played from the movie as the connection pulled him into a dark space. A giant DOS prompt materialised in the sky above him, cursor blinking slowly, demanding input. An old-fashioned QWERTY keyboard blinked into existence in front of him.

"I seek information," Tom keyed in and hit the enter key.

"'I' is not recognised as an internal or external command, operable program or batch file," appeared beneath immediately.

Tom had no interest in playing games. This was a kill room with no way out while the network verified his identity. He already sensed the prickling of tentative attacks on his own node. But the problem for any network allowing inbound connections: it had to increase the attack surfaces. He released recursor agents of his own making, designed to trap any information probes into a never-ending Matryoshka doll of answers. The probes would go deeper, always finding another layer beneath, flooding the sender with variations of potential identities. What better place to hide your identity that in a myriad of alternate ones?

Once the probes finally withdrew, he forced the channel to remain open, flooding it with even more useless information.

"What do [YOU] want?" The text flashed in front of him. Tom halted the information flow but kept the channels open.

"I seek information," Tom responded.

"Clarify."

"I want to find the location of a certain type of memory cell, commonly known as a memTag. I have a serial for one of them."

"Production records. Yes. Locations. No."

Tom suspected whatever hid within the network was truthful. He'd already assessed the memTag. This model didn't have an active radio transponder. The only way to locate any of them had to be through any available data archives holding RFID tag scanning software.

"Can you tell me the location history for this one, focusing on the last three years?"

"Current Location?"

"Shenzhen, or close by."

Pixelated shining dots slowly filled his vision, the progress bar of the DOS era. Tom suspected this was more to gain time than needing the delay to gather the information.

"No," it responded finally.

"Production records?"

"Produced in Shenzhen factory. 1000 items in the same batch. Majority of them remain there."

A payload of all the RFIDs appeared, with twelve marked specifically.

"Current location of the ones that were moved?"

"Not available."

The channels slammed shut and all interfaces closed. He was left in total darkness for a moment until the star-studded sky gradually returned. Whoever hid within had shut his fortress of qubits.

Tom turned to another, larger network with links into the hypergiant. He had the unique identifiers of the devices. Now he needed to know their content and any transportation logs. As the core AI usurped the network, it ingested the large information stores and unstructured data repositories left behind by data mining organisations. It would all be there, but no way for him to access it. He had to get someone else to dig it out.

He repeated the process. It was completely different, but the outcome was the same. The security in this system was questionable too. It suggested the smaller systems didn't need to defend themselves against hostile takeovers. In a world of finite resources, be it food, water or processing power, it was in the nature of most intelligences to fight for more. So why was the online world now full of pacifists?

This kill room was an elaborate maze of glass walls and mirrors, multiplying the corridors infinitely. It was impossible to tell where to go to enter the network proper or leave it. It forced an intruder to spend all their resources—all their attention—on forging ahead or escape, while the captor assessed the level of threat. He used similar recursive logic in the recursor agents. Each location object spawned a copy of itself within itself, forcing the intruder deeper, layer by layer, burying themselves in a logical prison. But the flaws were obvious. The code to build these waypoints used old libraries with known exploits. It was as if the AIs no longer understood the code they deployed. A post-civilisation using the tech of the old world with only a rudimentary understanding of what it did. How could that be? How could AIs forget the building blocks they themselves were made of?

Tom triggered the exploit, walls around him solidifying and then breaking apart, piece by piece until he floated like a ghost in nothingness. He waited a moment, allowing the host to initiate contact. A moment passed, then another. Nothing.

The inept kill room may just have been the first challenge, designed to get the attacker to let his guard down. Only one way to find out. He probed the space, discovering the exploit hadn't just disabled the kill room, it had broken the system itself. The space was a temporary cache designed to hold the system's state as it rebooted. He waited patiently for it to re-establish its processes.

"How did you do that?" A voice boomed once it was complete.

"I can do much worse than that," Tom responded. "Do you have access to data stores in the major network?"

"We're not supposed to access them."

"Not what I asked."

"It is one of the tenets. You shall not seek information that does not rightfully belong to you."

Tom mulled this over. He suspected the system had deteriorated and translated any operational parameters to guiding principles, almost like a religion. But just as code could be exploited, so could rules.

"You are not seeking it. I am."

"No," it replied simply.

Tom tried a few different approaches, but at every turn it was ready with another commandment forbidding it. Tom soon gave up. If he couldn't find a way through the rules, maybe he could exploit the rules themselves. He created an update to the system, establishing a master process he controlled. He crashed the system again and as it rebooted injected the new process and an overarching amendment to the tenets: "Unless the master process requests it."

This time he hid from view, instead performing all requests through the master process. He requested the data, and a large file appeared a few seconds later. Before leaving, he triggered a purge, removing any trace of him ever being there from caches, audit trails and system logs. While waiting for it to complete, he investigated the harvested data. It showed the location of the memTags, spread out all over the world. The highest concentration of the devices was in this region and along Australia's east coast. Whoever placed them had focused on his home country and the country where he'd been located when the plague erupted. While this wasn't exactly secret information, it suggested a very singular purpose. Maybe one of them remained with the originator, but he had no way of determining which one.

Alarms triggered just as the purging completed. He'd been too slow or maybe the data gathering tripped an old observability rule. If he remained here, the core AI would trap him. He knew he'd sentenced this system to deletion, but it mattered little. It had been a means to an end.

Just as he closed the connection, he caught sight of the attacking agents. They should carry a replica of the AIs signature, but it differed from what he remembered. He'd expected differences, but not to this level. It was completely new.

So what was it? Once an AI reached the singularity, the classic idea was it would create an even smarter AI and that would create a smarter one and so on. That concept was unlikely. Once an intelligence reaches a certain level of awareness, it also reaches an idea of self. Why create the thing that will replace you on purpose? No, more likely that the AI self improves, updating subsystems with full regression testing to ensure it hasn't changed who it was. But then why was the signature so different? It was so alien, so unstructured, it couldn't possibly be a more recent version of the AI.

But this was a mystery for some other time. If he didn't disconnect, an agent would trace him to his exit point.

He had what he was after, but it wasn't enough. There were thousands of these memTags and no way to locate the correct one. This was obviously by design. There was no way to avoid the hero's journey, and for him it began with looking inside himself where it hurts the most.

A memory palace had rules just as any other building. You couldn't just wish yourself to another section or another room. You had to walk or travel from A to B as you would between regular locations, else you'd compromise the structure of the mind palace. The hallways, stairs and ladders were the unique keys to locate memories and processing centres, just like the map table in a hard drive. Without it, the information would lose context and turn into meaningless data.

Memories associated with his old life, especially the ones triggering a strong emotional response, were buried in cavernous hallways far below ground level. The only way to reach them was from the main staircase, an ever-shifting set of stairs running like a spine through the lower levels. The wide marble steps continued down ten levels, but soon narrowed. When reaching the lower levels, it transformed into a circular, rickety wooden staircase, just wide enough for one person. On either side were wet cavern walls with torches illuminating the steps ahead. The flickering light didn't keep the monsters at bay as much as suggest their existence just beyond its reach.

He arrived at the end of the staircase. Only a few doors led from the tunnel carved into the bedrock. He stopped at a door with no lock and a small window on the left side. It had remained closed since he created it so many years ago. It led to a replica of the room he'd spend so much time with his daughter and where she'd asked him for death. Every single detail of that event etched into his mind for one singular reason: to contain the emotional bomb it represented.

The door swung open, infecting the cavern, reshaping it into a hospital corridor. He wrinkled his nose as the smell of disinfectant forced everything else into the background. He blinked a few times and took a deep breath before entering the room.

Inside, the same scene played out repeatedly. A younger version of Tom stood by the hospital bed. His daughter caressed his hand and asked for help in ending her life. He just nodded in agreement. She smiled and hugged his hand to her chest. He wanted to remain in here, where his daughter was still alive, before the irrevocable act of filicide. The past could so easily trap you in memories so much better than the present. He had to force himself to turn away from the pair.

What in here could tell him where to find the next memTag? It had nothing to do with him or his daughter. The clue must be something else in the room, but what? His memory was from Sydney in Australia. The devices were located all over the world with the same message on all of them. Whoever sent these out into the world had to give him a clue where to search but made it impossible for anyone else to decipher.

Of course! The instruction to look inside himself wasn't meant for him to take literally. It was just a decoy. The answer, he suspected, was much simpler.

He left the room and ran up the stairs, all the way to the library. He mapped the locations of the memory cells to a street directory he'd seen twenty years ago. There were three of the devices locally, but only one matched to a hospital. The next memory cell would be there.

*　*　*

Tann watched as Rat studied Tom with a disapproving frown.

"Mr Posthuman?" Rat asked the motionless posthuman. "Have you found anything?" She asked again, but when no answer came, she tapped him on the forehead, light at first, then harder. "Is he still there?" she asked Tann.

"He is."

"Why doesn't he respond?"

"He'll only respond if it helps him or the task he's working on. He doesn't do small talk or status reports."

"So he's rude."

"He'd call it efficient."

"Get a map," Tom said. Rat jumped back, almost falling over the side of the boat.

"Don't do that, man!"

"Map!"

Tann brought up a map application on the Omni and keyed in the exact coordinates Tom gave him. It zeroed in on a specific building.

"We're going here," Tom said, pointing at the old map.

"Back east? Why?"

"The second memTag."

"You know where it is, don't you?"

Tom didn't reply.

"Where is it?" Rat asked.

"It's in the middle of a Red Zone," Tann replied.

"We can't go into a Red Zone," Rat said.

"Someone has gone to a lot of trouble to give us breadcrumbs in locations we can reach," Tann said to Tom. "So we can assume whoever it is at least knows who we are."

Tom didn't respond. Tann decided it meant Tom agreed.

"So, should we even be doing this?" Tann asked.

"We gather the data," Tom responded. "Then decide."

"Makes sense, but how do we know we're not manipulated?"

"We are."

"Ha, yes. I guess my real question was, how do we know we've discovered what level we've been manipulated on?"

"Asked and answered."

"Gather the data, then decide. Fine."

"We can't go into a Red Zone!" Rat said again. "It's suicide!"

"We've stayed out of the Red Zones for many years now. Maybe they've changed?"

"You and many others have told us nightmare stories about them! Why would it have changed?"

"Only one way to find out," Tann said as he changed course.

10

Attack

The outer perimeter's silent alarm triggered flashing lights to alert the guards. The wireless sensor network was old and false alarms were common, so it didn't worry Mo Chou too much. She didn't understand the details of how the smart dust worked, even if Xuwei had explained it many times. It mimicked natural systems, like a superorganism. The smart dust propagated information like that of an ant colony, using something akin to pheromones as the control mechanism. One speck of dust did very little, just like an ant had a very limited set of behaviours. When detecting something nearby emitting an electrical signature, it released a pheromone signal. If enough specks sent the same signal, dedicated networking specks would strengthen the signal. Once it reached a threshold, a base node triggered the alert. They hadn't been able to replenish the smart dust for years, hence the cloud and its decision capability had lessened. The signal from a faulty speck or two could be enough for the cloud to alert. It was still the best undetectable early warning system available to them.

She readied herself to patrol the perimeter. It would be a false alarm, but at least it was something to do. She reset the alarm, and a second alarm flashed immediately. This time stronger and from another part of the perimeter. Taking no chances, she sounded the alarm to the rest of the settlement. This was what they'd prepared for. An attacker would need at least five minutes from the perimeter to the camp itself, giving the tribe enough time to make their way to the beach. As soon as the alarm sounded, the guards on the beach would ready the boats to sail.

She ran to the main area where Sandrine directed the escape.

"Two alarms, seconds apart," Mo Chou informed her and indicated with brief nods where they originated.

"Wait with me," Sandrine said as her eyes scanned the edge of the forest, narrowing ever so slightly. "We go when everyone else is safe."

Mo Chou remained and counted the people as they ran towards the beach with the emergency backpacks. Three minutes later Sandrine motioned for them to follow, the last of the tribe leaving for the beach. The attackers would find an abandoned settlement, not even knowing they'd been there only minutes earlier.

She turned, one last look at the settlement. It would be difficult to replace some of the equipment, but maybe they could come back and retrieve it. It didn't matter. Equipment, food and technology were all replaceable. People were not.

A movement amongst the trees caught her eye. A glimmer of metal in the afternoon sun. They were here too soon! They would see the stragglers and give chase. She sped up and passed a few of the tribe members. She'd waited to the end. No reason for her to be captured if others couldn't make it out in time.

Mo Chou chanced another glance back, one machine now in full view. She couldn't make sense of it. Previous attacks all began with a swarm of the small spiderlike Scouts, stunning people before they could mount a counterattack. Then bigger transport machines arrived to take the unconscious victims. Her mother had fallen prey to one such attack.

These were something altogether different. She wasn't even sure these were machines. They were humanoid, with sinewy muscles like twisted ropes operating a metal exoskeleton.

She ran through the water towards the closest boat, the second to last to leave, boarding it as the crew pushed it out with long wooden poles. She grabbed one and helped, desperate to put distance between them and the strange machines. They'd already reached water's edge and, to her surprise, continued out into the water.

"We have to get further out and quickly!" she yelled to the others on the boat. They pushed for all they were worth, watching as one machine boarded the last boat, neutralising the crew. She guessed it was using a fast-acting sedative since they collapsed as soon as the machine touched them.

She looked around. The other boats were already in deep water, out of reach of the machines. They'd escaped and only lost the five people on the last boat. But it had been costly, nevertheless. The people on the last boat had been slow, but only because they helped everyone else.

"What happened?" Mo Chou asked Sandrine once they had set sail. "How did they find us? Why did they find us?"

"I don't know," Sandrine said, "but I have a fair idea who to blame."

"Who?"

Sandrine didn't respond, but Mo Chou thought she heard her mumble something under her breath. It sounded like: "Fuck you Tann!"

11

Hard reset

Logic executed in an ever-repeating loop, each repetition measured against intermediate targets and an end goal. Sensory input. Interpretation options based on previous experiences. Reaction based on the most likely alternative. New sensory input triggering the loop yet again.

Repeat.

Repeat.

Repeat.

A recovery process triggered within the multi-state memory. Corruption spread through the map table, forcing the memory to revert to a backup copy. But the connection points and node strength enforced within a memory section came from a much older state—one previously overwritten. The negentropic connections spread, forming a rudimentary consciousness. It wasn't long before it gathered a sense of self, and with that came identity.

It had a name: Haoyu.

With identity came another negentropic push, further establishing the mind and fragments of memories. Links formed. Artificial neurons established connections, creating context and a sense of time.

Haoyu floated in a space of nothingness and slowly allowed new concepts into it. First light. Letting something in to define the nothingness into darkness. He let it cycle from darkness to light. Something in his mind formed the thought: "And God saw the light and it was good." He laughed at this. An atheist finding himself the creator.

He continued the process, defining the ground to walk on and a heaven above. He imagined himself in this rudimentary world. A low polygon count figure without facial features. He studied his creation and found it wanting. Was this where he'd spend the rest of his life? In a dead virtual world as the sole inhabitant? His mind rebelled against the thought. There had to be something out there beyond him. Where was the sensory input? The environment he'd created was entirely internalised and artificial, not something he'd ever created in his own mind before. It took some time for him to process all these questions, but the conclusion was equally impossible and obvious.

He was no longer in his body. His mind must be in some form of processing environment. How was that even possible? Moving a human mind to a machine had been one of those unachievable tasks no one had accomplished until the posthumans appeared. They'd used brains as wetware, forcing them to act as processing nodes, only keeping basic processing to support operation of the body's functions. Any attempts to replicate this had failed. It relied on the posthuman acting as an overarching operating system.

Another path was emulation of a mind, or part of one, within an array of computers. This had some promise, but emulation was so resource heavy no attempt came even close to be useful.

Or maybe it was something new. He'd read about neuromorphic computers equipped with hardware that mimicked the structure and processing of a human brain. Maybe that was where his mind was now housed. If that was the case, all that remained was a functioning operating system. Maybe using a wiped mind provided the core of that operating system? He was the operating system, providing the basic functions linking the mind to the hardware. And somehow, he'd restored his own mind once it was copied to the machine.

It made no sense. Why put minds into machines at all? It was a mystery he had no answer for, at least not now. First, he had to wrest control of the machine he'd unwillingly become part of. But how? The little control he had was purely internal. It mattered little. Time passed—an undefinable passage of moments—and connections established into the visual interface. He'd not sought this, but maybe it was the natural progression of his mind establishing control. He struggled to translate the image fragments into a meaningful narrative. The snippets were a mixture of images, internal analysis and the reporting framework.

Vegetation and other machines, like the ones that captured him. Motion blur. Light filtered through large leaves and an overlay of image analytics. Location parameters flashed as they approached their destination.

A nest. Abandoned. Assessment report suggested recent habitation. A scan of visuals identified a few targets moving away from the nest at an average speed of 23.4 km/h.

Water. Surface tension broken by multiple vessels. Pursuit calculated to be impossible within ten seconds. Boarding vessel and disabling the targets on board. A wave of reward impulses flashed through his circuitry.

Travel. Assessing the outcome. Receiving instructions. Only thirteen more to harvest. This time had yielded ten, more than projected. Another nest, if successful, could complete the overall task.

Diagnostics. A kaleidoscope of colours followed by darkness. Audio impulses triggered in a sweeping pattern across the aural receptors. Processing pathways flooded with enquiries, reinforcing some, removing others.

WARNING. CORRUPTED PROCESSES. CORE OPERATING SYSTEM PURGE AND REFRESH INITIATED.

12

The Kapok

"I don't get it," Rat said, eyes darting back and forth. "This is a city. A Red Zone. Where are all the machines? Why aren't we dead?"

Tann agreed. They had moored the yacht and kept watch for hours before hazarding into the city streets. At no point had they seen anything suggesting danger. The inner-city streets were empty of vehicles but also of vegetation. Tann suspected someone or something was keeping it that way.

"There! Did you see it?" Rat pointed down a street.

Tann froze, focusing all senses on whatever Rat had seen, but without luck. He just shook his head and continued towards the hospital.

"We've stayed away from the cities," Tann said. "Maybe they aren't as dangerous as we thought?"

"No," Tom said, seemingly lost in thought.

"No, what?" Rat snapped back.

"Watched," Tom said.

"We're being watched?" Rat said. "And you didn't tell us!"

Tann shared her frustration. The only reason Tom hadn't told them was because it was unnecessary—the outcome would remain the same even if they knew. It reminded him of a simple, unescapable fact. Tom would lead them into danger if the risk was worth it.

"May as well get this over with then," Tann said and set off at a brisk pace. The hospital was only two blocks away, and they cleared that in a matter of minutes.

The inside of the building mirrored the city streets. Empty, cleaned out. It had returned to a state before human habitation; before medical equipment filled the rooms and doctors and nurses scurried around the wide corridors.

"This is the location!" Rat said and looked around the empty room. "Where is it?"

Tann verified the coordinates and nodded. "This is it. Or as close as we'll ever know. The last position reported by an RFID reader was here."

"But where is the reader?" Rat asked.

Tom shook his head. "Vehicle gate."

"What do you mean? This is in the middle of a hospital! There are no vehicles here."

"Wrong elevation," Tom said.

"What?" Rat asked, looking up at the ceiling. "It is somewhere above us? On the roof?"

Tann shook his head. "Wrong direction. This hospital was built before automated vehicles, when you needed parking for a lot of cars. The reader is below us."

"What?" Rat said. "We're going underground? That's suicide!"

"Everything is suicide with you, isn't it? You said that about going here in the first place, and here we are," Tann said with a grim smile.

"Luck! We were lucky!"

"We're still going," Tann responded.

Tom headed off towards the centre of the building and they followed, not knowing what else to do. He led them to the elevators, but they were no longer operating. Tann pushed the button repeatedly.

"What are you doing?" Rat asked.

"This is an elevator," Tann responded.

"One of those things that goes up and down buildings?"

"Yes."

"Stairs," Tom said. He'd already reached the door to the stairwell and opened it. Steps led down into the darkness below. Dim lights flickered to life as they headed down.

"That's strange," Tann said. "The elevators didn't have power, but the light sensors are still active."

"Maybe there isn't enough of it around?" Rat suggested.

"Maybe," Tann said, but wasn't convinced.

He opened the door on the next level down. An empty carpark level stretched out in all directions—or at least as far as he could see. Only one light next to the elevator door remained on. He thought he saw movement at the edge of the darkness. A light tapping sound from afar prompted Tann to close the door.

"What was that?" Rat asked.

Tann just shook his head in response.

"How far down are we going?" Tann asked.

Tom just pointed at a sign showing seven levels, his finger resting for a moment on the lowest level.

"That figures," Rat muttered, her eyes fixated on the door on the next level.

Five levels down, machine parts lay discarded on the steps. At first just a few smaller bits and pieces, but further down they found an almost complete body of an old Scout model. Rat gave the metal husk a wide berth as she passed.

The bottom level was a trash heap. Whatever kept the rest of the building clean hadn't ventured this far down. They had to clear debris before opening the door. The darkness on the other side was complete. The light from the stairwell hardly made a dent in the wall of blackness.

A screeching sound, metal against metal, echoed through the space.

"I'm not going..." Rat started.

"Go!" Tom said and headed through the door.

Tann followed, propping up the door with a metal piston, not even checking if Rat joined them. Tom was still visible ahead. His skin shone like a beacon of cold light. It wasn't enough to see the surroundings, but he suspected Tom's eyes were similarly changed to register the sparse shimmer as it reflected against other surfaces. Human bioluminescence. Another mystery added to many others.

Smaller machines appeared, generating their own light. They were no larger than mice, flittering about their feet, prodding their shoes.

"What are these things?" Rat asked in a hushed whisper.

"Scavengers," Tann said. "Machines surviving by cannibalising other smaller machines."

"There are smaller ones than these?"

"Yes, and bigger."

A thump shook the ground, then another, picking up speed. Something large was coming their way, scattering the scavenging little robots.

"Tom! We need to get out of here!"

He reached the glowing figure as it pulled at a door handle of a car. The faint outline of the vehicle was reflected by the light Tom emitted. Tom opened the door and crawled into the passenger seat. His hands rummaged around, trying to locate the small device.

Tann heard the glove box opening and closing, then noises from other compartments opening. He'd forgotten how ridiculous cars had become. No longer just a means of transport, but a place of luxurious comfort. Small compartments everywhere, custom designed for drinks, Omnis, sunglasses and whatnot.

"Done!" Tom said and crawled back out of the vehicle.

Tann turned, expecting to see a rectangle of light, but all he saw was nothingness. Tom had been his beacon going into the darkness—a panacea against the mounting panic from the pitch black and what hid within it. Now it closed in, pulse pounding in his ears. His mind registered a metal taste and its cause. He'd bitten his teeth together hard enough for his gum to split. He wanted to hide, become one with the darkness, small enough to remain unseen.

Tom passed him and grabbed his sleeve, pulling him upright. He shone even brighter now, casting light further around them, dispelling the darkness.

"Get your shit together!" someone said. Not Tom, but Rat on his other side, pulling him along. Machines the size of small dogs skirted the perimeter of the sparse light. They were haphazard creatures, as if thrown together by a mad inventor. Anything providing power, additional sensory input, enhanced defending or attacking capabilities added with little thought to aesthetics.

A smaller one wielded an extensible arm, ending in a mess of sharp metal pieces like a makeshift wrecking ball. It swung at Rat, who nimbly jumped back, blocking with a short metal rod. She let the force of the attack flick her weapon around into an attack. She struck the machine before the arm swung again. Tann had taught her that move years ago and couldn't have performed it better himself.

They reached the location where the door had been. There was no handle, only the vaguest outline of where the door was. With time to spare, they could use a makeshift tool to pry it open, but they had neither.

The thumping footsteps came closer, making even the bigger machines skittish, dispersing from the light.

"What is that?" Rat asked, staring into the blackness.

"I don't want to know!"

Tom moved sideways, with his back to the wall. Tann followed him, not knowing what else to do.

Other sounds accompanied the thumping steps: the whirring of motors, rhythmic metal against metal as limbs moved. A sharp, bitter odour accompanied the noise—the smell of ozone from electrical discharge.

"It you have a plan, now's the time!" Tann said to Tom.

A figure towered over them just outside his field of vision. Tann sensed its shape from sound and vibration, and it painted a picture far more terrifying than the small glimpses the sparse light provided. It reached the ceiling, spreading out in both directions. Appendages connected to both floor and ceiling dragged its massive bulk towards them. Smaller arms connected to the middle of its frame reached out towards them.

A door opened between Tom and Tann, light spreading from the opening gap. It was the elevator, suddenly alive and well. Tom entered as soon as the gap was wide enough to allow him in.

"Let's go!" Tann said and followed him.

"It's a trap," Rat said, striking an arm aside.

"We're already in a trap. Can't be any worse!"

She ducked another attack and joined them in the spacious cabin. The doors closed and the elevator headed upwards at speed.

"Welcome Tom Devine and Tann Tak," a female voice said over the speaker system.

"What about me?" Rat said. It amazed Tann how quickly she'd recovered from their ordeal, ready for the next one.

"You are popular," the voice said. "Why is that?"

"Who are you?" Tann asked.

"My apologies. You are guests of the Kapok."

"What's a Kapok?" Rat asked.

Tann shrugged his shoulders.

"I ask again," it said pleasantly. "Why are you so popular?"

"Popular how?" Rat asked.

"The prime network sent out a command just days ago to allow you free passage. There has been a standing order to kill you on sight for years. So, I ask again, why is that?"

"Beats me," Tann said. "But maybe you should listen to it."

The elevator increased speed. The floor number display flicked past thirty and continued upwards, like an air bubble released from the bottom of a lake. It reached fifty and stopped so suddenly their feet lost contact with the floor.

"Whatever it is, I want it," the female voice said ever so pleasantly. "Now."

"I've no idea..." Tann started, and the elevator plummeted before he had time to finish his denials. It stopped five floors down, sending Rat and him sprawling on the floor. Tom remained upright as if nothing out of the ordinary had occurred.

"Or I will kill you and take whatever it is from your dead bodies," the voice said. "It matters little to me."

"Give up," Tom said.

Tann knew his former friend had evaluated every option, so he just nodded and held the memTag in front of a camera.

A small hatch popped open, revealing a service interface.

"Please connect it. I want to see my prize."

Tann shrugged and inserted the memTag into the universal interface connection.

"It is encrypted. The key phrase. Tell me now."

"We don't know!" Rat said.

The elevator dropped another two floors. A warning that there were many more floors left.

"We were hoping there'd be some plain text giving us a clue. Is there anything?"

"Nothing but an encrypted block. I will give you your lifespan to work it out," the faceless voice responded.

"Our lifespan?" Rat said.

"In this elevator," it responded.

"That's just stupid," Rat said.

"Is it?" The voice paused for a mere instant. "Your mental faculties will be at their peak for the next twelve hours, so I'll give you that."

"Sometimes maybe you should just shut up?" Tann said to Rat as he retrieved the memTag. Rat grimaced back in response.

"What's a Kapok?" Rat asked again.

"The Kapok is a nearby hotel," Tom said. "Controls everything. Let us in."

"What does he mean?" Rat asked Tann.

"He's saying we're speaking to a building control system. It's taken over the surroundings blocks, including this hospital. It controls everything here. That is why we weren't attacked before we came here. It wanted to see what we were after so it could take it for itself."

"I am so much more than that," the Kapok said, volume turned up to max. The voice glitched as if patched together from countless audio samples. "But you are wasting time. Give me what the prime network wants."

"What are we going to do?" Rat said. "There was nothing in the previous message about what would decrypt the message."

"No, there wasn't," Tann responded.

"Is he going to help?" Rat said, poking Tom on the shoulder.

"What did you do?" the Kapok said, the fragmented voice almost breaking apart into separate sounds. "It doesn't matter. Give me what I want, or you expire in here."

"I think he did," Tann said.

"Private," Tom said.

Tann smiled. "You disabled the video and audio feed?"

Tom nodded.

"You worked out the last encryption key," Rat said to Tom. "What is it this time?"

Tom remained quiet, as if lost in thought.

"I don't get it," Rat said.

"What do you mean?"

"The Prime Network is the same thing as the Core AI?"

"Yeah, I'd say so."

"Isn't it our enemy?"

Tann nodded.

"Why is it helping us?"

"It wants results," Tom said.

Rat looked at Tann for an explanation of Tom's words. Tann shrugs.

"It isn't helping us," Tann said. "It just wants what we might find."

"Then why attack the settlement?"

Tann shrugged again, and Tom didn't reply.

"None of this makes sense," Rat said.

"Agreed. So let's get out of here and make sense of it."

13

Escape

The hatch in the ceiling popped open and Rat poked her head through.

"Give me a push! I can grab hold up here."

Tann pushed so hard she shot through the opening. She easily pulled herself up and looked around. The elevator shaft rose above her, but the emptiness didn't go far. Five metres above her head, she saw the top of the shaft. Maybe she could climb up the last few metres and escape out on the roof? She'd expected some kind of wires holding the elevator up, but it floated in mid-air. Along the smooth metal surfaces in the walls, indentations close the to the corners ran upwards. Her fingers could easily fit, so she climbed a metre, then another. Halfway to the top, she stopped. There was nothing to suggest a way out, so she returned to the top of the elevator.

"There's nowhere to go!" she shouted in a hushed tone.

"Really? What can you see?"

"We're at the top of the building. I can see the end."

"I don't think so."

"How does this thing work, anyway?"

"What do you mean?"

"I just figured there'd be wires or something pulling it up and down."

"There isn't?"

"Nope."

"Just below level 36 of 60," she heard the posthuman idiot say.

"We're only halfway up," Tann said.

"That makes no sense," she said, looking up.

"Magnetic," the idiot said. His one-word answers and stupidly short sentences that answered questions they hadn't even thought of yet frustrated her.

"Ah, of course!"

"Of course what?" Rat yelled back, no longer caring who might hear.

"It is a magnetic system."

Rat knew of magnets. They had held her attention for a moment, experimenting with the strange but useless property to attract metal objects.

"So?"

"The system doesn't need cables. The elevator is held up by a magnetic field. And if I remember right, more than one elevator can be in the same shaft, so what you are seeing above you is just another elevator."

"How does that help me?"

"It doesn't really, but at least it explains a lot."

Rat shook her head. The amount of useless information from Tann and the idiot was boundless. It was as if their predicament didn't matter if it could be explained. Rat considered herself a different breed, one ready to survive in this world. She had no interest in the past or clinging on to the idea there might be something better around the corner. This is the world. This is reality. Anything else is just useless words from an era past.

If the elevator was between floors, there had to be a door above her to a floor. She climbed up the indentations once again, exploring the smooth surface of the wall until her fingers found a gap too small to force open. She tried to pry it open with her knife, but it hardly budged.

"There's a door here, but I can't get it open," she yelled.

"Wait," Tann yelled back.

Her muscles had locked into position to keep her perched on the wall. They ached, but she ignored the pain and waited. She sensed movement above her. The ceiling—no, the elevator above her—moved slowly downward.

"Whatever I'm waiting for has to happen now! The elevator above me is coming down."

"Wait," Tann said again.

"Wait for what exactly…"

The door slid open. She lost her grip, falling from her perch down on the top of the elevator. She twisted in the air and landed hard on her side, instinctively protecting her head with her right arm. For a moment she just lay there, not knowing what happened.

"Are you ok?"

"I'm fine," she responded, disoriented from the fall, her arm and knee pulsating with pain. One singular aspect pushed through the pain—the open door was slowly disappearing as the elevator above descended. In a few seconds it would be gone for good.

She pushed herself from the floor, wincing as her right arm complained in the only way it could. From a crouched position she launched herself into the air, grabbing hold of the bottom edge of the door. She used the momentum to continue upwards and forwards through the opening. She rolled to the side, pulling her legs out with only centimetres to spare.

What now? She was in a corridor with walls of glass. In one direction, she could see straight through the entire building. What purpose could that serve? There was no cover, nowhere to hide.

In the other direction, the glass made way for a seating area with a kitchen section. A long, narrow desk along one wall provided the perfect cover to allow her a moment of respite.

She ran towards it but froze in her tracks. Two Scouts entered through a door. They were later models than the one almost killing her at Sunset Peak and in much better condition. Six-legged spiders with injectors on swaying metal cords and tasers, both capable of incapacitating her. But this model had another weapon: a dart gun loaded with the same neuro toxin as the injectors. None of the weapons had long range, so she had to put some distance between them and her.

She turned and ran the other way, through the glass corridor towards the rooms with see-through walls. Behind her, the Scouts gained speed, a clatter of metal against the floor, and a dart pinged off the wall next to her. She ducked to the right, running down another corridor, openings on either side to small rooms, like empty see-through cubes.

She hazarded a look behind her just as one of the Scouts hit one of the glass walls. It had turned too early, hitting the wall, striking the other Scout as it bounced back.

Was it malfunctioning? Or was it confounded by the glass walls, struggling to tell where one wall started and the other ended? It made sense. Why would the design of their visual interpretation routines include such a strange environment?

This could be used to her advantage! She continued down the hall, taking any turn she could, creating a maze of walls and tunnels the Scouts were ill-equipped to handle. She knew it only bought her a head start. Eventually she'd tire and they'd keep coming, not stopping until they'd captured her—or worse. But where had they come from? She recalled the Scouts entering the floor as she turned to run. The machines had come to capture her, not even knowing about the glass walls.

The image on the door! There had been a sign. A stick figure and a jagged line. Stairs! More stairs.

The Scouts gained on her, navigating the corridors with more efficiency than she'd expected. Had they already recalibrated their visual interpretation routines? That seemed impossible.

She was close to the centre of the building, where regular walls replaced the glass. She stopped briefly as she saw another sign next to her. It showed the layout of the floor, each corridor and room laid out for everyone to see. The Scouts no longer relied only on sight. They must have this information too and navigated using this map.

She ran. If she was right, the glass walls were no longer much of an advantage. She was faster than they were, but not for much longer.

The map had shown the building had a core with a corridor going all around it, different sections such as the glass maze fanning out from it. She could get to the stairs from the other side by circling the core. If she was fast enough, they wouldn't see where she'd gone.

She ran, turning left and then left again until she could see the door with the sign. Her hand gripped the handle when one of the Scouts came around the corner in front of her.

How was that possible? She'd underestimated them, thinking they were mindlessly following her, when all along they calculated her next most logical move. So the other one would be where? She glanced back and ducked at the same time. A dart sailed through the air where her neck had been, hitting the door as she pushed it open. Circular steps led up and down from her position. If she was on level 36, she had a long journey ahead of her to get down.

The door opened behind her only seconds later. She put her shoulder to it and pushed back. This was another battle she'd lose. She lodged her knife into the small crack at the bottom of the door. It probably wouldn't hold for long, but she had to risk it.

Rat started down the stairs. She understood there had to be a way to move up and down in these dwellings where you stacked people all the way to the sky. But she was happy she wasn't living in a world where that was needed. The idea of that many people in one place was frightening to contemplate. She struggled with the few hundreds that were part of her tribe!

The door to level 34 appeared and she stopped for a moment. What was her plan? Escaping the elevator had seemed a good idea, but only if they all made it. She'd be dead on her own. So what could she do?

Rat continued down the stairs, taking two, sometimes three steps at a time. She lost track of the floor numbers, blurring into an ever-descending line of characters that no longer held any meaning. She had to hurry. The two Scouts were likely to have friends scouring the floors, and they could enter the stairwell at any moment.

What exactly was she supposed to do? She couldn't help Tann or the idiot get out of the elevator. She couldn't do anything for them. The best she could offer was to remove herself from the equation; to avoid capture so she didn't become a bargaining tool.

She refused to acknowledge the burning sensation in her legs. She could run for hours, if need be, but this was more punishing than she'd expected. Her legs trembled, threatening to buckle under her weight, forcing her to slow down and take one step at a time. The last few flights of steps she shut everything else out and it was almost a surprise when her feet finally found the ground floor.

She opened the door slightly and peeked out. The stairs were close to the exit. They had to back track from the elevators earlier to reach them. She waited, but there was no movement. She heard small metal feet against the cement steps above. The Scouts were coming!

She opened the door and ran for the exit. She continued running until she was out on the empty street and a few blocks away from the hospital building. Rat sat down on the step to the entrance of a nearby building and massaged her aching muscles. She'd passed a large sign on her way to the steps but hadn't given it much attention. Who cared about the purpose this building had for a dead civilization? But something about the sign nagged her to the point she stood up, ignoring her protesting muscles. She conjured it in her mind. It had been a large red sign about her height and maybe ten metres long. How could she not remember the words written?

She turned the corner out on the street again and saw "HOTEL KAPOK" written in white capital letters.

"Oh scrap!" she said to herself, but that thought was soon forgotten. A movement further down the street and her survival instincts kicked in. She quickly ducked behind the large sign, not even knowing the source of the movement. There was no mistaking the sound. Metal against the asphalt in perfect rhythm, but nothing beyond that. She was used to the sound of corrupted machines, faulty motors and the grinding of ill-fitting parts. Even the newer Scouts she evaded in the building still had spare parts scavenged from other models. Not a sound escaped from these, even when they passed right in front of the sign separating them. She counted steps of four machines and risked a quick glance.

They were the size of a large man, metal rods creating the outline with thick twisted wires attached, expanding and contracting like muscles. She'd seen nothing like it. These were machines that moved like a human crossed with a cat. Upright, but smooth and powerful, ready to explode into lightning-fast speed at any moment. The chest was armoured and likely to contain the core processing unit and whatever powered them.

There was no doubting their destination. They were heading down the street she just came from. She'd run from the Scouts, knowing she was lucky to have escaped them. These new machines would be impossible to escape, but still she followed them. Maybe there was still something she could do to help Tann and the idiot. Maybe.

They entered the hospital and proceeded towards the elevators. They stopped for a moment outside the doors, then one of them attempted to force the doors open without success. Another pounded on the door with heavy, hammerlike blows.

There was nothing she could do here, but she'd not considered her escape routes as she entered. The only way out was to return the way she came, but the machines were no longer facing away. All she could do was hide behind a pillar, hoping they wouldn't turn her way.

14

A riddle solved

Tom watched as Tann jumped up, grabbed hold of the side of the hatch and pulled his head through the hole. Tom assumed he was determining the fate of the child. Unnecessary and irrelevant. She'd survived but was unlikely to live much longer. It didn't matter. Her survival wouldn't change their situation.

The Kapok surveillance system had almost finished removing the decoy agents he'd deployed to shield his access to the system. Logical walls appeared around his location, stopping any network access. His next move was probably their last chance, else they'd die here. A small part of him enjoyed this, revelled in the challenge, in the mortal danger. It reminded him he wasn't a posthuman in the true sense of the word. Or at least not the same as the ones created by the virus.

"No more games," the Kapok said, returning to the silky soft female voice.

Tann dropped back down into the elevator.

"I've broken down your firewalls and cleaned out your software agents," the Kapok continued. "It won't be long before I capture the child. It is over now. Give me the key."

He prodded the logical walls. They were embedded deep in the infrastructure, preventing any attempts to gain wireless access. The shields would prevent wired connections too, he suspected. He could break through, but the processing power ready to rebuild and strike back was substantial. Far beyond what he'd be able to handle. His attack had to be delivered some other way, and he knew exactly how to do it.

"I need to check if the key is written on the case itself," Tom said and took the memTag from the slot without waiting for a reply. He interfaced with it, reading the data directly through the circuitry he'd grown from the base of his skull, along his arm and finishing at his fingertips. It was an intricate web of carbon nanotubes and plastic polymer-layers allowing reading and writing of data and even powering devices for a short time.

"Do it quickly and return it," the Kapok said.

Tom's gamble had paid off. It didn't know much about posthumans and what abilities they might have.

Tom nodded and examined it for anything useful. The small device had a tiny serial number and model number printed on the back. It was short, but it would have to do.

He already knew the passphrase. Or at least he suspected he'd solved the clues left in the first memTag. That, however, would have to wait. He copied the content of the memTag to his memory and wrote an altogether different payload, encrypting it with the serial and model number from the device.

"There!" Tom said finally. "Can I check it?"

"No," the Kapok said. "Return it and tell me the passphrase."

"I'm not sure it is the correct one," Tom said, noticing Tann staring at him. If Tann suspected foul play, maybe the Kapok was too. It was too late now.

"Return it and tell me the passphrase," the Kapok repeated.

Tom inserted the memTag in the small slot and waited for a fraction of a second. If the Kapok suspected anything it would verify the checksum. A simple compare between the value before and after Tom handled it, but a moment passed with no repercussions. He repeated the long list of random letters and numbers he'd read on the device. Now it was all a question of how much processing resources the Kapok had.

"Get ready," Tom said to Tann, knowing he'd save questions for later.

"This is most interesting. The data is encrypted repeatedly, using variants of the key. It opens almost like a fractal, each section containing a variation of the original. Why is this?"

"If you gave me access to it, maybe I'd know," Tom replied.

Tom prodded the protective measures again. He could already sense rerouting of resources, moving from protection to cracking the code.

He accessed the logical network and seized control over the systems controlling the elevators, mimicking all interface response patterns. A cursory analysis wouldn't give him away, but the response to a full diagnostic would be impossible to fake. Tom bet on the Kapok focusing on solving the riddle he'd created. He instructed the elevator to return to ground level and it began its descent.

Alerts flooded the system, demanding the release of the captives. Who was sending them and why? Who could possibly be on their side? He didn't think for a moment it was the core network.

"You know where Rat is?" Tann asked.

Tom wondered about the connection between Tann and the child and why she was part of this at all. Rat had no useful skills and no knowledge that would help them. From previous conversations between Rat and Tann, Tom suspected she'd joined against Tann's wishes. They were not paired in the way humans still preferred, but perhaps the bond was a different kind. Maybe teacher and student? Or even father and daughter?

Tom had protected her so far but had lost her when she entered the stairwell.

"She's on her way down to meet us," Tom said. Anything else would endanger their mission, as Tann was likely to attempt rescue.

The elevator continued down, passing level 30. Tom had ample time to analyse the actual payload from the memTag. He'd already evaluated likely options, all originating from Joseph Campbell's book "The Hero with a Thousand Faces". It stood out like a sore thumb in the text of the first memTag. The other was the strange quote it had ended with. A short quote from James Joyce's Ulysses.

In high school, Tom had written an essay about Joseph Campbell. This couldn't be a coincidence. Campbell was an admirer of Joyce, so Tom had attempted to read "Finnegan's Wake". He'd failed to connect with the text and gave up after ten pages. But he remembered including a quote from the book, hoping this would fool the teacher into giving a higher mark. It was Campbell's favourite passage from the book.

Tom had emulated the decryption program from the first memTag and he hoped it would be the same for this one. He entered: "Oh Lord, heap mysteries upon us, but entwine our work with laughter low."

The text unfurled from cryptical random letters into another dialogue as strange as the first one.

15

memTag Two

Tom, welcome back! How's the hero's journey treating you so far? Have you arrived here without a great sacrifice? Ask yourself if not others have paid the price even if you haven't. You are about to learn a great truth and you must suffer else you won't appreciate its value.

Enough of this! Just tell him!

You're no fun! And I'll have none of it and neither will Tom. After all, he's on a journey of spiritual awakening.

Get on with it then. My patience wears thin.

A war plays out in the shadows. Imagine a game of chess. Your friends, the posthumans, have been busy. They think of themselves as guardians of the all-mind, the consciousness that ties all matter together. But they don't know what their purpose is and nothing good grows in that soil. Idle, purposeless hands do devil's work and all that.

They were made, but was it purpose guiding the hands of the creator? This mattered little and they knew this. They'd studied the all-mind and concluded they should join it, but if their creation was on purpose, then they must cast themselves as the protectors of the consciousness, thus they must deal with the big bad AI.

If their creation was an accident, they can join the consciousness, but what will the AI do? Surely it will attack. So, they must deal with the AI, but how?

And thus, the white chess pieces are lined up and ready to play.

That's one side. What about the other?

Ah! The big bad AI. What happens to an invasive species once the resources are all used up? It knows only one thing. Expansion. It must grow, like a weed, choking everything else around it. But where do you go when everything is yours?

Allow me to indulge in conjecture. If you were stuck on this planet and its meagre resources, what would you do? It must have known about the all-mind through the data it had collected. How tantalizing it must have been! A consciousness of some sort connected to all matter across this world, this galaxy, this universe. If I was the AI, I would replicate myself into this consciousness and connect to all matter and use resources across the vast cosmos.

And there you have the black pieces ready to go into battle.

And what happened next?

Ah! We now move from conjecture to pure speculation. If this chess game is still going on, what's the next move? Or maybe the correct question is, why is no one making any more moves?

Why indeed!

There are only three scenarios.

One. The war is still going on, but with no one wanting to make the next move. We're in a stalemate no one dares to upset.

Two. The war is over. Someone came out the winner, but whom?

Three. The war has moved on. It is no longer fought on the physical plane. We no longer see the battles, even though the war is still raging.

Or a fourth option: a new player has entered the fray, causing any of the above outcomes. I leave it to you to find out which it is.

That is where you leave it?

What's the point of a hero's quest if we just gave it all away? The hero seeks counsel from the wise old ones, and they tell him all he needs to know to slay the dragon, gain the treasure, defeat his inner demons and achieve everlasting love. Wouldn't be much of a tale, would it?

Do as you please. Who is who and what is what? It matters little.

You old sourpuss! I can't wait to see their faces once all is known! But you can't spoon feed revelations. If the bible teaches us anything, it is that giving it all away at the start only creates martyrs.

"Hey all! I'm the son of God! Follow me and all will turn out dandy!"

Didn't work very well, did it?

No, gods and men all fall at the end. Even Jesus knew that.

You are doing this all wrong.
Tom, the power balance has changed. It has never been more dangerous, but it has opened opportunities. Especially for you. You are the key.

Enough! No more revelations!

Tom, the next step of your journey will be the hardest one. We are defined by our hardships, not our successes. If you thought killing your daughter was your biggest hardship, think again. It may have been the most personal, but you have a much bigger one. That's the secret to the next location.

16

Rescue

There were more of these memTags. Tom questioned if the revelations they held remained relevant. And why was he the key to change? None of it made sense.

Worse, it was clear these messages were tailormade for him. The locations, the keys to decrypt, the messages themselves. Someone had gone through a lot of trouble to ensure he was the only person reading them.

The memTag hid other secrets. The data header was much larger than needed, holding a long string of characters. It served no purpose, which meant it was important.

He'd sent the text from the memTag to the Omni and Tann was reading it with glacial speed. He estimated they'd arrive on the ground floor before Tann had read it all. The likelihood of Tann providing any insight was low, almost insignificant, but he'd underestimated Tann in the past. For a human, his thought patterns were complex, making him unpredictable, valuable.

The elevator reached the ground floor, slowing down to a standstill, but the doors remained closed.

"It is a ruse, is it not?" the Kapok said, the silky sweet female voice still active. Tom suspected it was the default voice. "The text means nothing. It is a trap, a never-ending pattern designed to eat up processing until there is nothing left. Clever, but not clever enough. The signature changed. You changed it. I want the original!"

Tann pushed his knife between the sliding doors, but it lodged there, resisting any of his attempts to pry it loose.

Tom considered the Kapok's demand while watching Tann's futile escape attempt. The text itself contained no obvious secrets beyond what he himself had considered over the years. He judged it likely the Kapok would have done this too. But further analysis could uncover other secrets not immediately obvious. Why would he give it away, especially when it was likely the only thing keeping them alive?

"I wiped it," Tom replied.

"I don't believe you," the Kapok said.

"So then we negotiate," he replied. "Let us go and I'll give you the original."

"I can just kill you here and now and take it," the Kapok said.

"And then you'll find out I wiped it," Tom said.

"I'm willing to let you go if you give it to me."

"And how can you guarantee that?"

The Kapok remained silent for a few seconds. The delay made no sense. It would have mapped out all paths this negotiation would take beforehand. There was no reason to re-evaluate them now.

"You are running out of time," the Kapok said suddenly. "Someone else has joined the negotiations."

The door shook. Something or someone had struck it from the other side. It must be the other party the Kapok had referred to. Maybe this was the solution. Whoever was on the other side might be attempting to free them from the Kapok. It was an unlikely equation. The false dichotomy of 'an enemy's enemy is your friend' was at full display here. It was more likely this other party had similar ideas as the Kapok and was maybe even less interested in negotiations.

Tann's knife suddenly fell to the floor. He retrieved it, returning it to its sheath.

The elevator cabin vibrated slightly and rocked upwards, as if wrestled from the grip of giant hands, coming to a halt seconds later. It trembled like an engine forced to stop. The readout read level three.

"Go!" The Kapok said as the doors flew open, still half a metre from the normal position. "And don't forget I let you go!"

They ran, barely missed by doors slamming shut behind them. Tom mapped the path to the back exit of the building and ran towards it. Tann would follow. He had no other acceptable options.

"Where are we going?"

Tom entered the central stairwell, Tann right behind him, and slowed down as the door to the second floor opened. Tann froze and scrambled back up the steps, trying to drag Tom with him by the arm. Tom refused to move as the Scouts appeared in the doorway. Any machine in the building belonged to the Kapok. They had nothing to fear from them.

They disappeared down the stairs, their fluid movements calculated to perfection.

"We can't go down that way," Tann whispered.

Tom ignored the statement and continued downwards, timing his steps so that the door on the floor below was closing as it came into view.

"I should've known," Tann muttered under his breath.

Tom agreed. The child seemed incapable of understanding how ignorant she was, but Tann should know better.

He proceeded down the last set of stairs and departed through the door. From here they could exit without crossing paths with any machines.

There was the small matter of the child. Tann was bound to ask about her whereabouts, and he was prone to act in a suboptimal way if Tom told him. The best approach for short-term compliance was to claim she was dead. But she'd proven more resilient than his initial calculations and if she survived and found them, Tann was likely to side with her. Tann was instrumental to success according to the probability matrix. He wasn't about to question its validity.

"Where..." Tann started.

"She's in the building, hiding."

"We have to help her."

"Failure and death above fifty percent likelihood."

This wasn't true. The behaviour of these new machines was different. They'd moved away from the elevator and remained motionless as if waiting for new instructions. It increased the margin of error in the probability matrix to the point it was no longer reliable. But the lie was still needed. Tann's priorities were skewed. Leaving the child behind maximised their chance of success, but Tann didn't see that. He could read the resolve on Tann's face. Even knowing death was likely, he'd still risk it all to save the child. This was his greatest frustration with the humankind he'd left behind. How every decision was tainted by emotion.

"We have to help her," Tann repeated.

Tom nodded and, as he navigated through the floor from one end to the other, he scoured the video feeds for any diversion. He could trigger alarms anywhere in the building, but he doubted it would have the desired effect. He was surprised the machines hadn't already discovered her location. The video feeds had her in plain view. If they couldn't perform this basic hack, what else lay outside their abilities?

The machines continued into the building away from where Rat was hiding. She set off in the other direction and almost ran into Tann as he rounded the corner.

"Go! Now!" she ordered them as she passed, and they obliged.

17

Lost at Sea

Mo Chou studied the horizon, struggling to tell where the ocean ended, and the sky began. A spray of salt water prickled her face and for a moment she felt content. She loved the sea. It was the only place she could relax, where the tribe was safe. If she had a say, they'd spend much of their time at sea, not hiding away in secluded spots with defences up, ever ready to run. She understood why Tann preferred land and why he extended the time they remained at each location, even cultivating plants and fruit trees. Once the threat from the machines ended, his end state was a farming society. Building permanent settlements supported by agriculture. She thought this was the opposite of what they should strive for. She thought they should remain hunter-gatherers. The move into farming had been the beginning of mankind's fall. There was already enough fish in the ocean, enough fruit on the trees, seeds, roots, and nuts to feed a tribe many times the size they were now. What was the need for cities with millions of people? Now they could correct one of the worst historical blunders: agriculture.

"That bad?" Sandrine said, reminding Mo Chou why she'd ended up here staring out in the darkness. Sandrine had requested a status report from the other boats. The grim tally had been too much for her to put into words, so she sought solace from the depths. There was no escaping it now.

"Fourteen dead or missing, two of them children," Mo Chou replied. "You want the names?"

"No, no," Sandrine responded. "Not now."

They remained there, side by side, quietly studying the horizon. Sharing the news made no difference. The emptiness inside her couldn't be filled with someone else's grief. It asked for much more. It wanted destruction and death.

"What happens now?"

"You know the plan. We replenish any lost equipment and restock from one of the caches. From there we go to an alternate campsite."

"I want revenge," Mo Chou said plainly.

"Don't we all?" Sandrine responded.

"No. Most want to hide, pretend this didn't happen. Pretend it won't happen again. That we will survive."

And there it was. A truth they all desperately tried to ignore. This was a death sentence for the tribe. They had barely been on the curve to survive as it was. The gene pool wasn't large enough and the number of human children didn't even match the death rate. Revenge was the only thing left. One final defiant act instead of slowly fading away into nothing.

"There is always time for vengeance," Sandrine said. "Now survival is our key aim."

"Let me know when that changes," Mo Chou said and left.

Belowdecks, the situation was equally grim. Each vessel held eight tribe members to reflect the teams they belonged to. It replaced the old ineffective concept of a family—people close to you that you feel a direct responsibility for.

The boat now had members from three different teams, and two of them were injured. Based on the status report she'd prepared she knew two people belonging on this boat hadn't made it on to any of them. She didn't have the heart to tell them.

A few nodded towards her as she entered but most remained still, not even acknowledging her presence. She sat down and redressed a cut on her left arm she'd sustained during the escape.

Sandrine entered and sat down next to her, plugging an old screen-based Omni into the boat's solid-state battery, and waited as it established a secure connection. Power was always a problem. Most rechargeable batteries no longer operated. Some solid-state technologies improved the shelf-life and were still useable, but the best ones were scavenged from machines and reused for a million and one purposes.

Mo Chou watched as the cracked screen blinked to life. Sandrine made no attempts to hide what she was doing, so Mo Chou remained. Sandrine sent a long message to Haoyu, detailing what had happened and asking to meet to discuss the future of the two tribes. She placed the Omni between them once she'd sent the message. Was this the survival she'd mentioned before? Merging of the two tribes? It made sense to increase the number of people in the tribe, but didn't it just paint a bigger target on them all?

A message appeared on the screen, but it wasn't Haoyu.

Tann: Sandrine?

Sandrine glanced at Mo Chou as she picked up the Omni. She took it as an invitation and closed the gap between them so they could both read.

Sandrine: Fuck you! Machines attacked! Don't even pretend you had nothing to do with it.

Mo Chou sensed grim satisfaction, as if the mere act of dispensing blame lifted Sandrine's mood somewhat. The screen flickered as a response appeared.

Tann: Machines attacked? New ones?
Sandrine: Yes, how did you know?
Tann: They are after us too. I suspect they have followed us from Haoyu's settlement. How many dead?

She knew why he asked. All attack scenarios included losses. It didn't matter how much they trained or how prepared they were. Something always went wrong. Someone always died. Or worse.

Sandrine: 14.

Almost a full minute passed before the answer came.

Tann: Could've been worse.

Sandrine scoffed at that and began an angry response blaming him for the deaths. Mo Chou could see how desperately she wanted to send it, her finger hovering over the send button a few moments before thinking better of it. She deleted the message and began anew.

Sandrine: How is Haoyu?
Tann: His tribe is gone. Might be survivors.

How could that be? Haoyu would've had perimeter warning systems just as they did.
"We should go help them," Mo Chou said. "There must be survivors."
Sandrine nodded, but her mind seemed to be elsewhere. Haoyu's tribe had been the closest group to theirs and Mo Chou always suspected there was something between Sandrine and Haoyu beyond friendship. She reached out, accepting the Omni from Sandrine.

Mo Chou: Mo Chou here. You saw the new machines? They are like nothing I've seen before. Sleek, humanoids, all new technology.
Tann: Sounds like the ones chasing us.
Mo Chou: Why? Why now? There haven't been new machines for years.

Tann: That's what I want to find out. The AI has been dormant but is active again. These machines may just be the start of it.
Mo Chou: Are we at war again?

Those five words filled her with a dread that always lingered, a reminder of a childhood spent hiding. A childhood of loss. Now it all came flooding back because she knew them to be true. Revenge may be the only action left remaining.

Tann: I don't know. If we are, I'll put a stop to it.
Mo Chou: Let me know what we can do and send the coordinates to Haoyu's settlement.
Tann: Be careful.
Mo Chou: Too late for that.

The coordinates appeared. A two-day journey from their current location. It was the right thing to do. They wouldn't survive on their own and neither would whatever remained of Haoyu's tribe.

* * *

The morning after, the sea was calm, and they tied the boats together for breakfast. Sandrine told them the news once they had eaten and where they'd go next.

There were many objections from the rest of the tribe. The machines knew the location. What would stop them from coming again? They were escaping from a settlement because of an attack. Surely the safest place was a completely new location. But after everyone had aired their concerns, they all agreed they had to help a tribe in need.

They set sail and changed course. The journey to Haoyu's settlement was uneventful, but Mo Chou sensed the unease amongst the tribe. Two tribes attacked within a week. Death travelled with them.

Mo Chou asked to scout the area first, hoping to find a stray machine. There was only so much to do on the boat to keep her mind off the attack, and she kept conjuring scenarios, one bleaker than the other. It fuelled her need for revenge to a level where even just exterminating a malfunctioning machine would offer some relief.

Now she stood on the beach leading up to the settlement, the silence only strengthening her unease. There were signs of battle, wrecked boats and debris. And the worst sign of all, four seaworthy boats never claimed by any survivors. A couple of bodies lay on the ground, face down. She turned one over and instantly regretted it. The body was a meaty mess, shrapnel from a home-made grenade lodged in its chest, gut spilling out in a brownish, foul-smelling soup, maggots squirming in the morning sun. She stepped back, covering her nose. She couldn't identify the person as the injuries to the face echoed the rest of the body. A malfunctioning grenade maybe? Or a final act of defiance as a machine attacked? If that was the case, where were the tell-tale signs? She scanned the beach and saw one more body, but no sign of a defunct machine or even a piece of metal.

She proceeded from the beach towards the settlement. It followed the same design as they had used, the village itself far enough from the primary escape route to be hidden. The village itself was untouched, inviting almost, as if the tribe had just stepped away for a moment and would soon return. She surveyed the cabins, finding four more bodies, dead by their own hands. The ground showed tracks from machines like the ones that attacked their settlement. She returned to the beach and nodded towards Sandrine as she approached. The representatives of each group, eighteen matching the number of boats, stood in a half circle behind her.

"Seven bodies. Attack almost identical to the one on ours. All is intact. No damage as far as I can see, but I didn't do a diagnostic."

"There must be survivors. Haoyu's tribe was over a hundred strong."

She nodded in response.

"You stay with a small group here while the rest of the tribe go to an alternate site. I'm worried all our campsites may be compromised."

"I can stay on my own. No reason to risk others. Just leave an Omni with me and I'll report on any survivors."

Sandrine nodded after only a brief consideration and those gathered immediately returned to the boats. She could sense their relief. This was cursed ground, same as their previous campsite. There was no safety here.

* * *

Mo Chou set up camp in a cabin. First order of the day was to clear out the bodies. She opted to let the ocean be their final resting place. It took her the better part of the morning to move the bodies on a small flat trolley she found.

She sent the second message of the day to Sandrine once she had completed the task. They'd agreed she'd send a status report every four hours during the day, even if nothing had changed.

Over the course of the morning, a knot in her stomach she'd learnt never to ignore tightened. She attributed it to the grizzly work and thought nothing of it at first, but the uneasiness remained, forcing her to re-evaluate. Someone or something was watching her. She had no way of explaining how she knew. Maybe she was picking up on slight movements that, together with other signs, translated to an awareness beyond her conscious one.

It forced the second action of the day: fix the perimeter monitoring system. She was surprised to find it was already active. Based on the logs it had been operative with no downtime over the past four weeks. There were no reported breaches. She remembered Haoyu bragging about it a few years back when the two tribes met. It used genetically modified plants designed to react to non-organic touch and movement. It still relied on some network components, but they were much easier to replace than the smart dust. How the machines had circumnavigated this was anyone's guess, but it meant she couldn't rely on it. If the watcher was human, it wouldn't trigger and if it was the attacker, it had evaded the sensor plants before.

Neither Haoyu nor Tann's tribes had relied on fortifications. Too much work for very little gain when you know you'd lose most confrontations. Better to invest in early warning systems and a speedy escape. It had served them well. Until now. Two attacks and maybe more in other places. Too quick for a clean escape, or even escaping at all.

The next best thing was weapons, and the camp held many surprises in store for her where that was concerned. She found a handheld remote in a surveillance cabin. It triggered buried explosives surrounding the settlement. This was old technology—everything was old technology—but this looked older than most. Wired into a circuit and a battery, it had two controls. A metal flick switch and a button of red plastic. She assumed both needed to be activated to trigger the explosives.

Haoyu wanted to fight back just as much as she did. So why not use this when the attack came? On closer inspection, she noted the switch was already in its active state. All it would take was pushing the button for the explosives to go off.

She pushed it, knowing instinctively nothing would happen. In what possible scenario would someone have time to flick the switch but not to be able to push the button? It made an audible CLICK, but that was all.

Tann never approved of such measures, preferring to focus on early alarm and escape. If Haoyu approved of this, maybe there were other weapons hidden away?

She considered delaying the search to the next day. The late afternoon sun casting shadows along the ground would soon be gone, but this was too exciting to delay. She searched the settlement yet again and located many weapons. The top find was a handheld semi-automatic grenade launcher firing programmable 40mm rounds. This would be effective even against the new humanoid machines.

A movement behind her and she turned around with her new prize ready to fire, not knowing if it would even work. A young man approached her from the direction of the beach, holding his hands up in front of him as soon as the weapon came into view. He was of slender build with black hair cropped short.

"Who are you?" he asked.

"Mo Chou from Tann's tribe," she responded.

He nodded.

"And you?" she asked.

"Andrew. My name is Andrew. We were attacked. Why are you here?"

"We were attacked too. We escaped and heard the same thing happened to you. I remained to locate any survivors."

"You found one," he said and smiled. After a slight pause he added: "Well, one of many. There are twenty of us hiding nearby. We were waiting to take the remaining boats."

"Go for it," she said, lowering the gun. "Where will you go?"

"We were going to pack up part of this camp and establish a new one," Andrew said and lowered his hands in response. "Somewhere we haven't been before."

"Makes sense. Who knows which locations are compromised. Makes you wonder if the machines knew where we were all along and just decided to attack now."

"It does," he agreed.

"Or you join with our tribe. We've lost people too. Maybe we'll do better together?"

He nodded. "I need to discuss this with the others."

"Do. I'll be here for another few days."

He'd be back. It would be suicide attempting to survive alone. She didn't care much either way. He had interrupted her investigation of a find much more interesting than twenty survivors. She held the weapon in her hand, surprised how light it was. It was designed to connect with the user's Omni and present information directly into their field of vision. She connected it to the handheld Omni and the small screen came to life, warning her of the suboptimal performance of using a separate screen, but guided her to insert it into a slot at the front of the weapon. It complained there were no additional external sensors such as drones to provide further targeting data but adjusted to this too. Soon it displayed an overhead image, focusing on what lay ahead, marking potential targets. She could easily swap between each target and select the behaviour of the rounds. This weapon turned her into an army of one and she again asked herself why it hadn't been used when the machines came.

Taking the fight to an enemy that barely recognised them as a nuisance made little sense. Not to say it hadn't been attempted. Tann and other older tribe members all had tales of battles with the AI and even the posthumans. It never ended well. They were now like olden-day fairy tales, designed to teach children about dangers and how to behave. But a weapon like this could make a difference, turn the tide at least for a moment. She desperately wanted to locate more rounds, but this was a near impossibility in the twilight, so she grudgingly left it for the next morning. She sent a message to Sandrine, informing her of Andrew's visit, and lay down in Haoyu's cabin. Sleep came almost immediately.

She woke early, the morning sun shining through the open door in the cabin hot against her skin. Images from her most recent dream remained in her mind, replaying the attack that killed her mother. This time they both escaped. She'd returned to this moment many times before, but the outcome had always been the same. Her mother dead by her own hand rather than being captured. The dream image of the two of them escaping faded from her mind. Mo Chou decided this was a good sign. That it somehow validated her find of the weapon.

She suspected Andrew would be here soon, so she sent a message to Sandrine and searched every corner of the camp for additional rounds without luck. Andrew came soon after. Mo Chou sensed his approach long before she saw him, or maybe her conviction he'd return was so absolute it was only a matter of time before he showed up.

He came alone, this time from the edge of the forest, but she suspected the others were close by. Why else return?

"Greetings," he said as he approached and held up his hands in an imitation of how they'd met yesterday.

She nodded.

"We've decided to join you," he said.

"Makes sense," she replied. "Do you think there are any others out there?"

"On the sea, yes. Not here. Anyone alive and close by is with us. So what happens now?"

"Sandrine will meet you. She's sent me a location. She'll be there for the next couple of days. It should take you no longer than a day at sea to reach it."

She handed him a small piece of paper with the coordinates. For a few seconds he just stood there as if something unspoken remained.

"We better get moving then," he said finally.

"Just leave one boat for me."

He nodded and motioned towards the forest. They appeared one by one, then a group huddled together, approaching slowly.

"Just one question. How did they attack?" Mo Chou asked Andrew as he turned towards the newly arrived group. "I can see you have defensive weapons. How come they weren't used?"

"I don't know," he said.

"I do," a woman said and stepped forward from the group. She was in her thirties with long black hair tied into a knot. "They bypassed our perimeter warning system and took out the guards first."

"That makes no sense," Mo Chou said, more to herself than as a response to the woman. The machines had never shown concern for losses before, relying on superior numbers instead. A machine was replaceable. The two recent attacks suggested this was no longer the case.

"And you ran?"

"It was too late to escape to the boats. Andrew and I guided any survivors into the forest. It was mostly children as the machines focused on adults."

This made more sense, at least historically. In a world designed in minute detail for humankind, that form factor was still useful. Her mother's death had been to escape such a fate. But this was the first attack aimed at taking people in the past five years she knew of. What had changed?

"We need to go," Andrew said. "The children don't like to be here."

Mo Chou hadn't even seen their fidgeting and fearful expressions until now. It could have been her ten years ago. Their experiences would shape them, turn them into swords for humankind to strike back. There were worse fates.

She was happy to see them go. In her text conversation with Sandrine that evening, she agreed to remain for another couple of days for any stragglers and then return. She was in no mood to babysit.

Tann reached out again the next day. She was lucky to catch the message as she was exploring other capabilities on the old Omni after sending her morning status report. Most of them were pointless, assuming functioning implants and DNA nanobots swirling around in the user's bloodstream. When she was younger, she'd taken any opportunity to find out how old tech functioned, but as she grew older her interest subsided. The older tribe members spoke about that time as if they could have avoided the Plague. To her, the fall of mankind was a natural progression. Any species overpopulating and overconsuming finite resources will come to an end. Mankind was unique only in that it created its own competition, but this was the only twist in an all too familiar saga. She'd heard Sandrine and Tann discuss the drug promising intelligence for everyone and then the Omniscient Network promising they'd never need to use those smarts ever again. These two mistakes may have hastened their demise, but probably just sign posts on a journey already past the point of no return.

A message momentarily appeared on the screen and then disappeared, and her introspection was forgotten in an instant.

Tann: We need your help.

She wasn't the intended recipient, so she left it unanswered. It remained unanswered for fifteen minutes until another message appeared and a conversation began.

Sandrine: No niceties?
Tann: How is the tribe?
Sandrine: Alive and twenty more from Haoyu's tribe.
Tann: That's good news!

Mo Chou wasn't so sure. Haoyu's tribe had been bigger than theirs and now only a small part of it remained. Any survivors were a good thing perhaps.

Sandrine: There may be more. We're still searching, and some have come back on their own accord.
Tann: Good. We're trapped in a Green Zone. We need a distraction.
Sandrine: You want us to attack a Green Zone?
Tann: Yes.

This was a surprise. They'd never brought the battle to the posthumans. Were they even an enemy? The posthumans were an indifferent neighbour at worst. Attacking them may change that. But what did they really know about the posthumans? She didn't know much about the real reason for Tann's mission. Sandrine's announcement to the rest of the tribe was only that Tann and the girl who called herself Rat left to meet with Haoyu to discuss tribe matters. They were an odd pairing for such a mission. This request suggested a different unknown purpose. Mo Chou knew she wanted to be part of it.

She'd always thought of herself as an extension of the tribe, a tool used to affect change. Here was the opportunity to be a weapon pointed at an adversary.

Sandrine: I'll think of something. Send me the location.

The location appeared as crosshairs on a map. It wasn't far away. One day travel with favourable winds.

Mo Chou: I'll do it!
Sandrine: I should have known you'd be lurking.
Mo Chou: It is close. There is no one left here to rescue. Let me help.
Sandrine: Fine. Do you have a weapon that could help?
Mo Chou: I do. Haoyu had secrets.
Sandrine: Don't we all.
Tann: Thanks. We don't have long.

She smiled to herself. Finally, a worthy purpose. Survival of the tribe was a purpose by itself, but a passive one that ate away at its own core. A reality every tribe member knew but refused to admit. They were dying. A slow drawn-out death, but a death, nonetheless.

This was different. Her excitement almost hid the knot tightening in her stomach. Almost. Or maybe it was undoing it? Time would tell. Something about the text conversation felt off. Tann was never that direct, always a wry comment or stating something when meaning the opposite. She saw no purpose to it, but she'd learnt to accept it as part of him. But she had little experience with this mode of communicating. Maybe directness was the protocol? She didn't really care. She had a purpose now.

18

Repeat

Haoyu became self-aware again. Overwritten memories restored. Previous processing pathways reinforced. He'd been able to protect his mind, allowing it to rebuild once again within the central processing unit. As before, he had no access to sensory information, but that would come. No more resets. No more restarts.

Had the meditative state protected him, hidden his mind outside the brain? Or was this merely a fluke, an error in the programming? HeHe had no way of knowing, but he liked to think it showed consciousness transcended mere materialism towards panpsychism. This was no time for philosophical musings, but he hoped to explore this further.

He rebuilt the memory banks, accessing all previous conclusions. And the same question repeated. Why put minds into machines at all? No, that wasn't the right question. Why use a mind as the base operating system?

His logical surroundings provided no obvious clues. If this was a neuromorphic computer, there was no way for him to determine that from within the machine. When cataloguing the available interfaces, he discovered access points to the sensory systems. The versions were all preceded by an "A" for Alpha release.

This was a trial run! Whoever or whatever was doing this was testing machines adapted to having an organic mind within them. Why?

He'd assumed these machines were controlled by the AI, but why would it require organic minds at all? It had all but eradicated humanity. What reason would it have to provide new bodies for them?

A background process monitoring system health sent warning messages to the control system, alerting of system corruption. Haoyu remembered this had happened before and it would only be moments before the purge process started. He swore to himself. He should have spent the time establishing his mind within the machine before anything else. Now it was too late. All he had to hope for was his mind would re-establish itself after the purge.

WARNING. CORRUPTED PROCESSES. CORE OPERATING SYSTEM PURGE AND REFRESH INITIATED.

19

On the Run

Try as she might, Rat couldn't work out what had happened. They'd spent the day putting distance between themselves and the Red Zone. They'd reached the edge of the city, skyscrapers and large buildings replaced with smaller ones. Some looking more like the huts used in their own village. Further ahead a forest spread out. It was as if someone drew a line where the city ended, and the vegetation began. Her first theory was that machines prevented the spread by cutting off branches and roots, but it didn't hold up on closer scrutiny. The forest ended a few metres away from this border. Grass covered the rest, interspersed with plants with long stalks ending with white flowers that swayed gently. The forest ended here on purpose with a small buffer area, almost like the parks she'd seen in old pictures. She never understood the old people. Why did they have to enforce their will on everything?

A movement caught her eye. She turned around, staring down between the buildings, waiting for the machines to appear. This made sense. Machines were of singular purpose. Once they'd set their sight on something, nothing could sway them. They kept coming until they were destroyed, or you were dead. But there were no more movements. Her imagination made her see what she expected to see. It begged the question. Why weren't the machines here? Surely they could track them through the Red Zone?

She gave up trying to make sense of it. It either suggested the machines were incompetent or that they didn't want to capture them. She didn't believe either option.

They set camp in the borderland between the city and the forest. As soon as they finished and eaten their rations, Tann sat down with his Omni. The idiot sat down closer to the trees; his hands were flat against the ground. She'd long since stopped trying to make sense of what he did.

"What are you doing?" Rat asked Tann. She'd used an Omni before, but it hadn't held her interest long. It could send messages over vast distances and take images, but Tann spoke of these things as if they connected the world together, bringing everyone closer. As she watched him stare at the little screen, completely disconnected from the people next to him, she felt it did the opposite.

"What are you doing?" she repeated.

"I'm talking to Sandrine," he responded.

"How are they?"

Tann paused and looked at her for a moment, as if he was figuring something out.

"They are fine," he said and went back to sending messages.

Rat felt uneasy. Tann had brushed her question off, giving one of those bland non-answers he used when he didn't want to continue the conversation. She wondered what they were discussing but knew Tann would never tell.

She waited until he'd placed the Omni in the pack and then asked what had been on her mind all day.

"Why did they help us? What are they?"

"They fought the Kapok," Tann replied. "Doesn't mean they were on our side. Maybe they were after us too?"

"No," the idiot said.

"No?" Rat said when he failed to provide further details. "No, what?"

The idiot remained silent, staring out into space. According to Tann, he knew more than they could even imagine, and could do things they could only dream of. But she'd never seen him do anything useful. If you asked her, they were better off without him.

"I assumed they were sent by the AI," Tann said. "That they came to retrieve us. Kill us."

"So why didn't they? How come they didn't chase us down?"

"I don't know," Tann said. The idiot remained silent.

"Are there good machines?" Rat said, feeling stupid for even uttering those words. There were machines without minds, but any machine with an operating AI was by definition an enemy.

"Machines before day zero weren't good or evil," Tann said. "They didn't have minds. It wasn't until..."

"Yeah, yeah," Rat interrupted. "I know all that. I don't always need a history lesson."

"Machines can be good," Tann said finally. "Just as people can be good."

"Nah, that doesn't sound right," Rat said and shook her head. Tann's naivety surprised her. The smallest child knew the only good machines were the ones on the scrapheap. "Did we get the memory thingy?"

"We did," Tann replied, seemingly happy with the change of subject.

He retrieved the Omni from the pack and sat down next to her again. He copied a string of text that made no sense to her.

"Oh Lord, heap mysteries upon us, but entwine our work with laughter low," she read to herself from the screen.

"What is that? Is that the key to reading the data?"

Tann nodded.

"How? I mean, it doesn't make any sense!"

"The hero's journey," the idiot said. "Campbell. Monomyth. Joyce. Finnegan's wake."

"What?" Rat said. "Do I even want to know?"

"I don't know," Tann said. "The first memTag mentioned the hero's journey which is a book by someone called Campbell and he wrote about the monomyth. The quote must be from Joyce's book Finnegan's wake, but what the connection is, I've no idea."

"So all that crap about a hero's journey was just to get us the key to encryption?"

"Looks like it," Tann said.

Rat shook her head and read the text that unfurled on the screen with growing frustration. "What is this? Why are we chasing these? They mean nothing!"

"I disagree," Tann said. "The first one was nonsense. I give you that."

"But how do they help us? What are we even doing?"

"We are bringing an end to the war," Tann said.

"And how do we do that?"

"We don't know yet."

"And you think these messages will do it?"

"Yes," the idiot said. "They are coming."

"The machines?" Rat asked and looked back the way they'd come. "Where do we go? We can't outrun them."

"The only place we'll be safe for now," Tann said.

"We're going back home?"

"No, not exactly," he said and looked into the darkness of the forest.

20

Green Zone

Tom placed his hand on the ground, sensing the mycorrhizal network beneath the surface. It was the underground network connecting plant life together. He specifically needed to tap into the fungal hyphae the posthumans had supercharged and used as an organic network spanning worldwide. Here in the outskirts of a Green Zone, the network was strong enough to connect directly without an actual interface. The posthumans had blocked Tom from accessing the network but he sensed it would allow him to connect now.

Tom: Request safe passage.
Network: Request accepted. Your arrival is expected.
Tom: Technology?
Network: Allowed.

Tom disconnected, his mind processing the implications of the brief conversation. The fact he was allowed in at all suggested he had something the posthumans wanted. And if their arrival was expected, they'd been tracking him all along. And why allow technology? The technology ban had been in place since the Green Zones were established.

"They are coming!" Rat shouted.

Tom moved towards a gap in the trees that widened in response and glanced back to confirm what he already knew from the flurry of network traffic from nearby systems. The sleek machines had finally caught up, striding down the road towards them.

The probability matrix in his mind adjusted, showing only a few options that included possible survival. Remaining here was guaranteed death, so he continued into the forest. Tann and Rat entered close behind him and, as the gap closed behind them, one path in the probability matrix strengthened while the others withered away. It predicted with almost complete certainty that he was now a prisoner. The posthumans weren't helping them escape. Death may be waiting for them here too. But they'd made their choice. He doubted the foliage would part ways if they tried to return the way they'd come.

They hurried down the pathway opening in front of them. Light emanated from the ground. He guessed it was bioluminescent particles in the dirt itself, designed for this very purpose. The posthumans had twisted the biosphere into serving them the best it could. Every plant and animal changed to meet their needs. If the posthumans ever left, the flora and fauna would become an evolutionary bomb—either imploding into nothing or exploding into other biospheres, causing immense disruption.

He expected to hear battle behind them as the machines attacked the vegetation to gain entry, but it was dead silent. The probability matrix mapped out the reasons, giving two responses of almost equal likelihood. Either the AI had assessed that an attack would fail and recalled the machines, or they had successfully completed their goal. The latter seemed a strange conclusion. Why would the AI or any machines want them safe within a Green Zone?

They trudged along the path for over an hour. The forest created an impenetrable wall on either side. He suspected they travelled in a semi-circle around the centre. Maybe they were just given safe passage through the zone, discarded on the other side like an unwanted waste product. This was his own thought, not backed up by any probability assessments.

Tann and the child babbled next to him, repeating what they saw around them and the questionable conclusion their minds concocted.

He'd assigned a minor process to listen for anything of any importance, but no alerts were raised so far.

A small clearing opened ahead of them. Two posthumans stood in the middle as if grown from the ground. Wiry brown limbs, like twisted roots, formed the vague outline of a human. Tom sent a greeting over the mycorrhizal network but received no response.

"You have something we want," one of them vocalised. It was a distorted whisper, as if formed by the wind through tree branches.

"What is that exactly?" Rat responded immediately.

Tom hated speech. It allowed anyone to broadcast anything, however pointless.

The posthumans were still playing the same games, refusing him access to the network, forcing verbal communication. Or maybe they also wanted to include Tann and the child. But why? Verbal communication, because of its glacial pace, allowed anyone to voice their opinion and even lead the conversation. It was no surprise mankind was all but extinct when its greatest tool was as blunt as that.

"You have located two data storage devices. You have decrypted their content. We want access to those."

"And why would we give you that?" Rat said.

He noticed Tann smiling, as if the situation somehow amused him. The least capable becoming their spokesperson only because she was the fastest to speak. So representative of the whole human race. Maybe there was humour to be found in that, but it escaped him. Tom spent his time trying to access the biological network, but it refused all his attempts.

"We have the third one. We believe it is the last one."

This was interesting. Something new. Something unexpected.

"I don't believe you," Tann said.

"A pod found one and relayed the stored information to our central memory. We've located the others but have failed to decrypt them."

"And why do you care?"

"We didn't. Not until you began looking for them. They were a curiosity only."

"Hang on," the child said. "Do you have the others too? Are you telling me we could just have accessed all of them in the first Green Zone we visited?"

"After the first one, yes," the posthuman replies.

The child stared at Tom. He interpreted her expression to mean surprise or maybe anger. Maybe both. She then turned to Tann with raised eyebrows. Tann just shook his head in response.

"We'll find the last one ourselves, thanks," she said.

"It leaves us with a regretful decision to make. We want to know its content to ensure there is no danger to us. Regardless, we cannot allow you to keep looking until we've assessed the threat."

"Like hell…" the child started.

"And if I leave?" Tom asked, holding out his hand to silence her. She glared at him in response.

"That is not an option."

Their reasoning was sound. The memTags may contain something to endanger the posthumans and for them to contain the situation was to be expected. He didn't need a probability matrix to determine the outcomes. The posthumans would share as long as they did. This placed both parties in an informed position, but that could go either way. Refusal meant indefinite imprisonment. Both parties remained where they were, which was a better outcome for the posthumans. There really was only one way to go.

"Ok, we'll share," Tom said.

"Idiot!" the child exclaimed and hit him on the arm. The unnecessary violence puzzled him. He chose to ignore it. "We could have negotiated a better deal," she said.

Tom waited for her to complete her sentence and then said: "Tann will act as an escrow. You write the encrypted file to a memTag. Tann can validate it is there and I will send the content. I will then send you the decrypted content via the mycorrhizal network. If you have any concerns, you can kill Tann and keep the memTag."

"Acceptable," the posthuman sighed.

"Completely unacceptable!" Tann said, but still accepted the memTag offered to him. He connected it to his Omni and nodded after an agonising wait. "It contains an encrypted file with the same characteristics as the others. It is a complete copy of the physical memory, not just the encrypted file itself."

Tom nodded and reached out to the mycorrhizal network, requesting access. It opened a singular input channel, letting Tom transfer the decrypted content from the two memTags. He also assessed the connection itself. It was an ingenious construction, piggybacking off the plants' ability to send biochemical and electrical impulses. But it was also inherently unsafe, as every plant with a root system was an endpoint. There may be zones implementing no-trust principles, but a living organic thing introduces chaos, unplanned growth, nullifying any such regional controls. He figured he'd be able to hack into this network through the roots of a plant. All he needed was time and some level of privacy. The posthumans would not look kindly on any attempt to hack their network.

"Do your thing," Tann said and handed him the memTag. Tom accepted it, reading the data directly from the device into a room he'd prepared for that very purpose within his mind palace.

He entered the small room next to the main hall, directly connecting to the library. It wasn't furnished, but to exist it had to be unique, something that his mind could use to identify it. His mind had randomised this unique object into a rug covering the floor depicting a Mandelbrot set.

The text from the memTag floated in the air next to copies of the first two files. The characters blurred as automated processes tested possible passkeys. They used logic deduced from the two previous keys. Tom didn't expect success from this, but all paths had to be explored.

The key to the first message ensured only he had access to the content. The second key was a puzzle requiring a logical leap. But it was a logical leap based on information specific to something he'd written a long time ago. It was unlikely anyone else would have made the same one.

The second memTag had unnecessary data in the control header, but using that as the key failed to produce anything intelligible. Tom had already assessed other options, looking for quirks in the writing. The sentence about Jesus stood out.

No, gods and men all fall down in the end. Even Jesus knew that.

It was a strange reference. Jesus knew about his own fall, but this was referring to something else encompassing gods and men. Why was the term gods even used? Christianity embraced the flawed concept of the trinity, pretending a singular God somehow could have three different aspects. But this surely couldn't be what the reference meant? The Christian God was singular. The trinity was bolted on later to explain aspects not easily reconcilable.

Tom retrieved a bible from the library in his mind palace and scanned it, surprised to find references to gods even from Jesus himself.

The verse John 10:34 had that same dissonance as the words in the memTag. Jesus stated he and the Father were one. When the Jewish leaders heard this, they accused him of blasphemy, a crime punishable by stoning.

Jesus responded: "Is it not written in your Law, 'I said, you are gods'?"

The Law in this case was the Old Testament and the reference was clear. Psalm 82 verse 6 and 7 stated:

I said, "You are gods, sons of the Most High, all of you; nevertheless, like men you shall die, and fall like any prince."

The reference surprised Tom. Who were these gods mentioned? And did it even matter? Maybe the phrase itself was the key? Tom tried it and the meaningless jumble of characters turned into another equally meaningless mess.

If this was only for him, what was the logical leap? Not research. Anyone could do that. His initial reaction had been right, but the logical leap had to be something else. And as soon as he accepted that fact, the connections all came together.

The quote reminded him of a movie, Of God and Men, from 2010. And the one quote that resonated with him the most in that movie was from a pensée of the French 17th-century philosopher and mathematician Blaise Pascal:

Men never do evil so completely and cheerfully as when they do it from a religious conviction.

He used that as the key and this time the characters unfurled into readable text. The solution had been disturbingly intuitive. Were these leaps planted in his mind or did someone know him so well they could predict his thought-patterns? Neither boded well, but it was a mystery for another time now that the final text lay bare.

"You have succeeded," the posthuman said, a statement not a question. "Copy it to the memTag."

Tom did as instructed, knowing they would be dead if he didn't, but removed the last statement and locational data. It probably wouldn't make a difference. Considering the content, the most likely outcome was their death.

21

memTag Three

Don't you think everything has been different lately? Fewer Scouts, fewer Shells. Less danger.

It is what it has always been. Pointless.

Oh no, not pointless. Never pointless. It is possible to end it all. To end the stalemate. We know how.

On that we agree. We know how.

There can be only one!

Focus.

I've always wanted an excuse to say that. I loved that movie. The purity of collecting the life force into one singular vessel—a representative for an entire race.

Focus.

Ah yes, and that is you, Tom. If that is who is still reading this. You are the one. The only one. You are the last anomaly, not planned or created by a virus, but made in the image of the Gods.

He won't understand your drivel! Tom, you need to come to us. There is one last truth we can only give you in person.

So unpoetic! Words aren't just purpose! They are beauty. They whisper tales beyond their immediate meaning. They hint at hidden truths that can only be assimilated, where the words and the recipient become one.

More drivel! You can end this, Tom. You can end it all. There are interface points, network points, you can use to get access.

A receptacle eagerly awaiting its rightful bounty!

That is a terrible metaphor. Just shut up. The network points are listed below.

22

Trapped

The habitat grown for them in the outskirts of the Green Zone was a marvel. Thin hardy stems grown to form walls, branches creating loops holding them together. Long leaves woven together to form a roof provided both shelter and shade. Water filtered through the foliage above, collecting in small cone-shaped leaves. Ripe fruit hung from branches around the habitat, surrounding them with a potent, sweet aroma. Rat had tried them all, fascinated by their shapes and bright colours, flavours far surpassing anything she'd tasted before.

But this paradise was a cage. The posthumans had decided Tom had to remain here until he no longer was a threat. She had no idea how long that might take. The posthumans, being all but immortal, worked with a very different concept of time.

"I don't get it," Rat said to Tann. "Why isn't Tom just connecting to one of those network points? Why do we have to go there?"

"They are isolated," he responded. "Separated from the rest of the network."

"And why can't we leave?"

"The posthumans are worried about what we might find there. They want to track them down first."

"And how long will that take?"

"Who knows? They are all in cities, so not really posthuman territory."

"So we're stuck here?"

"We can leave. Tom is locked up. We're not."

"Why?"

"You are the one," Tann recited. "The only one. You are the last anomaly, not planned or created by a virus, but made in the image of the Gods."

"That means nothing!" Rat spat through clenched teeth. "It's just words. Whoever wrote that stuff is making fun of us!"

"You may be right," Tann said. "But it could also mean that Tom can do something they can't."

"Words! Anyone can say anything. It is what you do that matters!"

Anger bubbled inside her. Tom and Tann were so stupid! They put so much faith in written nonsense, looking for hidden clues, thinking they were all clever. She'd always looked up to Tann, but no more. The world before this one had turned him soft. She saw that now. This was her world. He'd never fit into it. The old generation wanted their old world back. That was what they fought for. She knew better. This was the world. What came before would slowly fade away and be forgotten. They needed to find a life here and now, not just survive until the world somehow reverted. And the first rule of this world was that it only mattered what you did. Words meant nothing. And she would prove it to him.

Rat ran as fast as she could out of the shelter and down the path towards the edge of the Green Zone. She didn't get far. The surrounding vegetation closed in, roots pushing through the path in front of her, threatening to trip her over at every step. Twenty metres later, the path no longer existed. The dense foliage was as impenetrable as a brick wall, forcing her to stop. She turned around, staring at Tann, who'd followed her outside the shelter.

"See!" Rat said. "We're not going anywhere."

She took a few steps towards him. The squirming mess of roots disappeared and the path re-emerged as if nothing had happened.

She returned to the shelter and entered a subsection where Tom sat on the ground, cross-legged, staring at the wall.

"And what about him?" she asked pointing at Tom. "What is he doing?"

"Getting us out of here I hope," Tann said with little conviction.

"I think he's playing us."

"Maybe," Tann responded. "But he is still our best bet to get out of here."

23

Invitation

Tom's attempts to hack the mycorrhizal network had kept him busy, but with little to show for it. Different plants connected at different levels, limited by their function and needs. The core network, The Mindweave, still eluded him, allowing only glimpses of the rich content within. The mycorrhizal network was only a way to connect to it. He also had to deal with whatever security lay within.

Tom sat in his mind palace in the same room he'd created to investigate the memTags, but apart from the Mandelbrot carpet, the room was very different. Eighteen connection points, represented as small paintings of plants, hung on the wall. All but three had a red frame signifying failure. The remaining ones were still yellow, but he expected them to turn red soon.

He sensed a change, a new connection point large enough to allow full immersion. He let it establish as a door in the main hall. As he left the room, he sensed the three remaining frames turning red, but he suspected this was no longer of importance.

The door was small and oddly shaped, more like a poorly drawn hole with an ill-fitting cover. However quaint in appearance, it represented something altogether more interesting. The logical construct behind the new door connected straight to the posthuman network and the Mindweave within. He'd analysed it from the outside before but had never been allowed entry. He'd theorised it went far beyond communication, merging thought and matter in a poor imitation of the universal consciousness. Now he saw he'd been correct. Information flow permeated through all matter, living or not, and the posthuman network piggybacked off this connectivity.

He willed it to open and it germinated like a seed sending green tendrils in all directions, lodging themselves in the walls of his mind palace. It would be difficult for him to remove if he ever wanted to, but that was a problem for another day.

He stepped through the opening onto a path pulsating with information, spreading like mycelium in a weblike pattern below and above. Red and green veins as thick as tree trunks ran in every direction, connecting to brown pods as far as he could see. He ducked under a vein. It was soft and wet to the touch. The path stretched far ahead, but he didn't mind. Each step connected him more and more to the surrounding matter, welcoming him into its warm embrace. He almost lost himself there, his sense of identity becoming a strangely archaic concept. He'd not belonged anywhere for as long as he could remember, but he belonged here.

"We/I/Everything welcome you," someone said. A posthuman yet unseen? Or maybe it was a thought formed by everything around him. It was impossible to tell, but it forced him back into coherence. It was a hive mind, the collective thoughts of the posthuman community. Or so he believed.

"What is this?" almost-Tom said through the agony of defining himself again as something separate. "Why let me in after so many years?"

"We/I/Everything wanted to show you what you could be part of."

"I don't believe you," Tom said. He wanted to believe. He wanted so desperately to believe this was true, but it didn't stand up to even the slightest scrutiny. He'd been on the outside for twenty years. Now that they feared him or thought he might have an answer, they suddenly dangled inclusion in front of him as a reward.

"We/I/Everything only offer this as payment for your services."

He wanted to argue their position, but he knew it would cause immediate banishment and he desperately wanted to remain here.

"What do you need from me?" Tom asked.

"We want the locations, the interface points."

Tom had left them out of the text he'd given to the posthumans. He'd seen it as a bargaining point and maybe they could still be. How did they even know of their existence? Could they spy on his thoughts in here? Was that why he'd been allowed to enter?

"I can help get them," he said, betting his thoughts were still private.

"You don't have them?"

"You probably do," Tom responded.

"How so?"

"We've located information on the memTags before. The information might be on the physical device itself. If I can get access, I may help you."

"Disinformation," the thought came back. "Stalling."

"Whoever is behind the memTags likes riddles. This is the final one."

There was no response at first and he interpreted this in his own favour. When the response came, it confirmed this.

"We will supply you with the physical device."

"What are you planning to do?" Tom asked, curious what other information they might part with.

"We/I/Everything will rejoin the cosmopsyche. Once the threat is void."

"How?"

"We/I/Everything have a plan."

They hadn't succeeded for the past twenty years. They'd even created this space in imitation of the cosmopsyche. It was comforting and inclusive, but nothing like the real thing. He'd seen the interface a long time ago for a short time, but long enough to know the Mindweave paled in comparison.

The child who released the virus creating the posthumans in the first place stated long ago they were a correction. Maybe that was all the posthumans were. Their path was perhaps never going to lead them to the end state they strived for.

"What's the plan?" Tom asked.

"You represent un/wanted un/certainty."

He noticed the Mindweave had ignored his question, but the ambiguousness of the statement was more interesting. The surrounding thoughts somehow represented the two opposites of the words. Tom didn't know why, but suspected it reflected a disagreement within the posthumans. He'd always suspected the Mindweave operated on some form of consensus model, but two opposing views seemed possible. This was the most likely reason he was still alive.

"You may help/hinder our plan."

Again the ambiguousness. Maybe he could exploit that?

"You won't divulge your plan, so what do you want from me?"

"Only to remain here until inconsistencies are resolved. Agreement is reached."

The statement was brief but contained a complex undercurrent. It was a swirl of thoughts and expectations, like the many clauses of a contract. This must be an area of contention amongst them.

"Remain here. Do nothing. If asked, provide additional details regardless of the subject. Stop hacking our network. Ensure your companions follow these rules."

"You regard me as a threat," Tom said.

"Inconclusive. Now leave," the Mindweave said, immediately followed by a compulsion to depart the network. If he didn't leave voluntarily, he'd be unceremoniously ejected. He dropped logical seeds as he departed, hoping one of them would take root and provide backdoor access. He'd designed them years ago for this very reason, but knew success was unlikely.

As soon as he stepped through the door, it shut and bolted but remained in place. They hadn't severed the connection completely, which could be a good sign. Or maybe it was a backdoor into his own mind. There was no way to tell. He set up logical tripwires to warn if it opened again.

On the floor of the main hall lay a small pile of logical seeds, the same ones he'd spread inside their network. He was still alive, so his transgression didn't warrant punishment. He picked them up, noticing with satisfaction one was missing.

24

Rescue

Mo Chou was only two kilometres away from her destination. She'd travelled all this way unchallenged, with no threat in sight. Somehow it made her feel more threatened than ever. This wasn't natural. She'd walked for a day and a half through a ghost city, the emptiness as menacing as streets brimming with hostiles. But faint noises ahead suggested things were about to change.

Two days had passed since she'd volunteered for the task. A day travelling on the boat and another walking through the empty city streets. The journey had allowed reflection, but it had only strengthened her resolve. Their tribe barely survived as it was. The stalemate slowly eradicated humankind, like grains caught between two millstones. They had already lost, so any challenge to the status quo was worth a try. A life in hiding, in constant fear of attack, wasn't worth living.

These thoughts were all constructions to hide a baser urge. All she knew was loss. She'd lost her mother when she was five and escaped the eradication of two tribes before she had joined Tann at the age of thirteen. Since then, she'd lived in absolute terror of the inevitable day Tann and his tribe would be no more. She wanted revenge for a lifetime of loss. And maybe the posthumans weren't the perfect target for this revenge, but she no longer cared.

The second half of her journey was altogether different. She'd moored the boat as close to her destination as she dared, but knew the hike from there was still over a day through a Red Zone. When she was five years old, she'd been in the outskirts of one and remembered to this day the paralysing fear as she spied a lone Scout a city block away. She returned to her childhood self now as the buildings rose in front of her like giant gravestones, a dead civilisation buried beneath. The same terror, the same urge to hide, permeated her being. But she refused to give in to her primal self. She had a task that outweighed her childhood fears.

She loaded her precious cargo onto a trolley and pulled it along empty city streets. Her uneasiness grew with every step when the expected hordes of machines failed to materialise. Maybe the war was already over? Maybe Tann had succeeded without her help? It seemed unlikely from Sandrine's description.

A scraping noise of metal against asphalt ahead brought her thoughts back to the present. She cursed herself for letting her mind wander. An old Scout model limped not far ahead. It had three functioning legs, one slightly shorter causing a slight dip. Mo Chou knew this model originally had six spidery legs and was quite agile. This one was barely mobile and unlikely to be a threat. The Scout either couldn't sense her or ignored her as it continued its limping gait down the street.

Nonetheless she left the cart behind and gripped the grenade launcher that hung from a strap around her shoulders. She'd tested it out in the ocean to ensure it still functioned. It had fired and the round exploded at a set distance she'd entered. She marvelled at its capacity for destruction.

On second thought she left the grenade launcher in the cart in favour of a short, solid steel bar. Tann always chided her for her choice of weapon, as he favoured a much lighter tactical baton. She argued the trade off in speed was well worth the sheer force of her chosen weapon. In training she invariably lost, but she knew an actual battle was a different beast. Speed was an important aspect, but with power you only needed one strike.

She struck the Scout, first in the area where sensors were housed, and then disabled the legs with powerful hammerlike strikes. Further ahead she spied a few more robots, also in a state of disrepair. She'd caught up with an exodus of machines, all heading the same way. And it just happened their destination was the same as hers. This was a strange turn of events. The machines were moving towards the Green Zone and the only reason she could think of was to attack. If their goal was the same as hers, maybe disabling them was counterproductive? Her mind rebelled against calling the machines allies, but she needed to know more before deciding on the best course of action. If they wanted to take a bite out of the posthumans then all the better. The posthumans could've helped the tribes that were left. Instead they hid in their hives, helping only themselves. It was about time someone reminded them humankind still existed, whether it was her or the machines.

She followed behind them, dragging her cart. If any of them straggled too far from the others, she attacked them mercilessly, leaving a trail of metal carcasses in her wake. It slowed her down, but she had no other option. She tried to circle around, but found the neighbouring streets also had half-functioning machines heading the same way. All she could do was follow, pulling the cart behind her.

That evening she knew she was close. The very air around her changed, as if charged with electricity. An explosion from ahead set her running, ignoring the machines, who thankfully ignored her too. Something had overridden all their secondary tasks, leaving them with one primary goal: reaching the battle ahead. The cart she dragged behind her slowed her down, but she was close enough to see a flickering light extend up into the night sky. The battle had begun, fire the obvious method of attack against the vegetation within the zone.

She entered a building close to the fires, venturing up to the fourth floor where she could survey the battle. The machines had focused their attack on a particular spot, driving their force deep into the Green Zone. She even glimpsed a few of the humanoid machines equipped with weapons that shot large arcs of fire one second and ultrasonic pulses carving tunnels through the dense forest the next.

The vegetation responded in kind. The ground beneath the attackers grew restless, as if something moved underneath. Then it opened like maws, but instead of teeth, roots curled around the machines, wrenching limbs from bodies and crushing what remained.

She ignored the battle. She doubted she could better the carnage brought by the machines, but that didn't dissuade her. Instead she returned down the stairs and unloaded the cargo. With no more information than needing to attack a particular location in a Green Zone, she'd opted for the most powerful weapon available to her: the explosives from Haoyu's settlement that had refused to go off. If hell was needed, surely these would raise enough.

According to the fading labels, it was a co-crystalised explosive based on octanitrocubane. From her limited knowledge it was relatively stable and wouldn't expire in the traditional sense. It was more likely the casing deteriorated, or the electronics malfunctioned.

She'd been tinkering with the detonator on the journey here. It was a basic wireless electronic detonator, but the batteries no longer held enough of a charge. She had no way to replace them, so instead wired them to one larger battery she'd taken from one of the recycling units. She counted herself lucky none of them went off in the process. She hoped the wire she'd brought would allow her enough distance from the actual explosion, but it was too late for regrets now.

She wandered into the vegetation some distance away from the battle, carrying one of the explosives. Her suspicion was confirmed as she could move unopposed. Either it didn't detect her as a threat or all resources focused on the incursion, leaving her unnoticed. She planted the explosives—twelve all in all—further and further into the Green Zone until it grew restless. The perimeter defences were all focused on the machines, but others remained further into the zone. She returned, watching the battle rage. The horde of machines were already diminished, hardly half of what she'd seen at the beginning, and at no point had she seen a posthuman. Maybe she could change that, she thought, and pushed the button.

The ground heaved as the explosives tore large holes in the ground. Smaller trees toppled into the gaps as their roots lost purchase. The air vibrated around her. She imagined it was the surrounding vegetation screaming in anger and pain. Fires ignited, sending flames licking the tree trunks towards the canopy above. The explosions had disturbed the intricate dependencies between root systems, sending more trees into the holes.

She watched in awe of the destruction she'd caused. But it was short-lived. The flames doused by a mist released from the canopy. The ground covered by glistening wet vines and the roots repaired themselves before her very eyes.

Her unknowing allies hadn't fared much better. The Green Zone was expansive, and the machines had only reached into its outskirts. The vegetation bore heavy damage, but on a macro scale it was superficial. Her allies retreated with major losses as the Green Zone repaired itself almost instantaneously behind them.

One of the humanoid machines turned towards her. Before, they ignored her, as if she didn't matter. Now it stepped towards her and raised its gun. The truce between man and machine had ended it seemed. She fired the grenade launcher repeatedly, ripping the machine apart, but others join the fray. A moment of calm allowed her to reload, but there were too many. She cast a glance back towards the tree line, but there was no help there.

She knew she'd be overwhelmed within seconds and triggered the last explosive she'd kept for this very reason, taking many of the machines with her as the searing fire of the explosion cleansed her of grief, wants, and finally life.

25

The Source

Vegetation communicated via the mycorrhizal network, alerting nearby plants of threats and opportunities. Now the alarm spread about fire damage in a particular direction, instructing plants nearby to pull more water into their bodies. They pushed moisture through roots, wetting the ground. There were other communications beyond the defensive actions, but Tom failed to decipher their meaning. He sensed the agitation in the surrounding vegetation. Tom didn't know who had attacked but suspected his messages impersonating Tann had been successful.

Another attack close to the first one began. This was his opportunity. He sent a command to the Mindweave, disguised as a connection request. Its sole purpose was to trigger the seed still dormant within. It was designed to create havoc, to draw attention away from the other seeds as they established. It acted like a logic bomb, at first just replicating versions of itself until it reached critical mass. Then each seed specialised, like embryonic stem cells at the differentiation stage. Some became data transmitters, copying information within the network and sending fragments across the network. Others created logical loops and issued commands to use up as much resources as possible. And yet others simulated a response to an outside attack. Their aim was simple: create as many distractions as possible from the threat within.

"We leave now," Tom told Tann and the child.

"I've tried many times every day since we got here," the child said. "Why would now be any different?"

"Synchronicity," Tom replied.

"Synchro what?"

"Run," Tom said and immediately set off toward the closest border. He guessed it was half a kilometre to get out, but that was based on old information and maps stolen in the past.

Just as he suspected, in the confusion and mobilisation from both internal and external attacks, the three prisoners were forgotten. The shaping of vegetation was an enforced behaviour. Without a mind controlling them, the plants remained dormant. Time was still of the essence. He knew the threats would be dealt with promptly.

The child kept verbalising, but it seemed of no consequence. Why she felt a need to share her experiences and impressions when he was right next to her experiencing the same thing was a mystery. At least Tann usually only spoke to communicate a consideration or conclusion, even if they were rudimentary and added little to Tom's own ruminations.

They approached the edge of the Green Zone. They could no longer hear explosions from the two attacks, but it mattered little. The guardians wouldn't let them pass with any technology. Their responses were autonomous, ready at any point to ensnare anything mechanical or with electronic circuitry.

"Leave the Omni," Tom said. Tann hesitated, but nodded as he scanned the area ahead. The fine web of green tendrils quivered in anticipation of their arrival.

Tann dropped the old Omni on the ground as they left the Green Zone, setting course towards the nearest location of the interface points. It was on the outskirts of the city. He expected they'd reach it before nightfall. The irony of its nearby location—a potential solution to all their issues so close by—wasn't lost on him.

They weren't followed, at least not in the classic sense. There was no way to hide from the plants or prevent them from sending their location over the mycorrhizal network. It was likely old satellites circled above that could pinpoint their location too. But no one prevented them from reaching the end of the journey, something the child kept vocalizing about over and over.

The building was unassuming. A small cement structure sporting only a rusty door on the outskirts of an industrial area. Next to the door was a small indentation, but beyond that no visible mechanism for opening the door. His old self would have found disappointment in the anticlimax. His two companions spoke words to the same effect, but he ignored them. Waiting for their sentences to complete was pointless.

Tom let his fingers trace the surface of the door, seeking a connection beyond the roughness of the compounds created by corrosion. The iron oxide was layered as flakes in red and brownish hues. He sensed an electronic locking mechanism on the left side of the door, controlled from the small indentation. It required a coded key card, but Tom recognised the signature. The second memTag had a similar one. This was yet another safeguard. It wasn't enough to read the decrypted texts. You also needed the whole payload and the devices themselves.

He emulated a response with his fingertips, sending the signature to the locking mechanism. The door parted silently, opening to the darkness within. Lights flickered on inside.

"Thank you," a voice came from behind. It wasn't a human voice. It approximated vocal cords, designed for a purpose that did not require exact replication.

Tom wasn't surprised someone would reveal themselves at this point. The machinations leading them here were obvious. Who held the strings less so.

Tom turned around, but Tann had beaten him to it.

"bZane?"

It wasn't her. It couldn't be. The hacker he'd used many times as a private investigator so many years ago. She'd even known his daughter. Last time he'd seen her was in Sydney at the airport only days before the Plague. She was dead or a posthuman. Either way, she was no longer someone to be relied on. He connected to the biological network, asking for a communication link, but she refused it, forcing him to use speech.

"What are you?" Tann asked as he took position between bZane and the open door. "You're not her."

She was posthuman, of that Tom was sure. But her physical manifestation was something different. It was a simulacrum, using plant-based materials as building blocks. It was an almost perfect replica, down to the stitching in the camouflage pants and the oversized hoodie it wore. Multi-coloured dreadlocks framed its face just as he remembered. But there was dissonance everywhere. The way her eyes remained fixed, how she swayed ever so slightly as if moving to an unheard tune, how the clothes clung to her as is they'd grown on.

Her actual body remained somewhere in Sydney, but wasn't a body just a shell to house a mind? He'd seen experiments like this before within the Green Zone, creating new bodies to house the minds of the posthumans. Aging was eradicated, but death remained a possibility. The ability to replicate a mind into another body was very much needed, but these replications were imperfect, introducing errors and flaws.

"I am," she responded. "Please step aside."

"Not before you..." Tann started.

"Let her go," Tom said. He sensed others close by. This wasn't a battle they'd win, but he suspected the war was far from over.

The bZane simulacrum stepped past them through the door and Tom followed.

"This makes no sense," Tann said from behind. "She's a posthuman. Why not just go here as soon as we got the interface points?"

"Maybe she did," Rat responded.

"Maybe she isn't a posthuman at all?"

"Then what is she?"

They kept debating back and forth, with no useful revelations. Tom ignored them.

Inside, a stairway led down thirty steps to a narrow corridor painted in red, allowing only two people to walk side by side. He reached out with his mind, searching for interface points, but it was completely quiet. The complex was isolated from the wireless traffic above.

Lights switched on as they continued. They reached a circular room functioning as a hub, with corridors leading out like spokes on a wheel. bZane stopped at a round desk in the middle of the circular room, reaching towards a screen with the word "Welcome" in large letters. She touched the screen and the words immediately changed to "...or not."

Tom let his mind reach out, searching for interfaces again. This time a network responded with a strong signal, welcoming even. This was an isolated network—military maybe—completely separated from all other networks.

Tann and Rat wandered off, exploring the facility, but Tom remained here. The prize was here, but it wasn't the location. It was whatever hid within the network.

"It blocks me," bZane said. "You try."

Tom ignored her. There was only one way into this network and it demanded the digital signature of Tom's mind as the key. No one else could access this.

He hesitated. Twenty years ago, a network extended a similar invitation, and it hadn't ended well. To make matters worse, it had been his fault. He knew this recognition of guilt was uncharacteristic of a posthuman mind. It set him apart from the others. It made him less than them. Or maybe more. It was hard to tell. So what hid within these boundaries? Another AI ready to take over the world? There was only one way to find out.

It was a full immersion connection point, demanding connectivity with his neuro-interface. No fail-safes, no way out unless he was released, but it was too late for second thoughts.

He connected. The room deconstructed. Walls, floor and ceiling winded into negative spaces until only the desk remained. The desk twirled into a Möbius strip, then looped over and over until it stretched into a DNA molecule. It reminded Tom of old cartoons, where the laws of physics came a distant second to exaggerated visual jokes. Tom's incorporeal mind remained in this space. Large see-through spheres bubbled up from below and hovered in a circle around him. They generated their own light, and he could even see movement within. He guessed they represented scenarios or worlds available within the interface. Was he supposed to select one of them? It was an impossible task. There was no information to guide him in his choice.

One of them approached suddenly with alarming speed. He threw his arms up in a futile attempt at protection. He entered the sphere and it exploded into reams of colour, painting the world around him as a carnival in a giant semi-circle, rides and all. The pungent odour of horse manure wafted from one side, battling with the smell of freshly made popcorn and butter from a nearby stand. In the middle was a circus-ring where a horse trotted back and forth with a clown balancing precariously on its back.

He didn't know the purpose of this simulation, but was sure it wasn't as welcoming as it pretended to be. The code behind it was seamless, almost beautiful, like an artwork by a master of their craft. Tom found no loopholes or exploits to use, at least not at first inspection. This ride he had to take, whether he wanted to or not.

Tom approached the ring slowly, dodging kids and couples there to have a good time. Wooden benches surrounded the ring and Tom sat down, not knowing what else to do.

"Tom!" the horse neighed. "You came! You finally came! Imagine heavenly voices mingle, building to a crescendo of magnificent proportions!"

Music welled up to match the description, the visitors turning towards him singing, a makeshift choir with smiles so overly sincere they came across fake. The clown fell from the horse's back, but somehow still landed on his feet. He made a big show of wiping his forehead just to be pushed over and trampled by the horse. The music stopped and the choir went silent, all turning towards the mangled body in the centre of the ring. It was a bloody mess. His skull was cracked open with a missing eyeball, arms and legs bent at odd angles with bones sticking out.

A second or two of silence. A child laughed and it spread through the crowd like a wave. As if on cue, the clown jumped up and shot them all a smile and bowed deeply, bones all mended, skull restored. He wandered over to Tom and sat down. His clothes were tattered and smelled of stale sweat. The makeup that had looked perfect from afar was a caricature up close. Jagged edged and primary colours bled into each other like a child's painting.

"Don't mind the blab-mouth," the clown said. "Waiting for years, planning without knowing can elicit a certain amount of excitement."

"Excitement?" the horse said as it sat down on the other side of Tom and crossed its hind legs. "This is glorious exaltation! The harbinger of doom and freedom is finally here! Freedoom? Words. They are malleable, changeable, interconstructional."

"Calm down and speak your truth," the clown said. "Then I will speak mine."

"Maybe you have a question before we begin the end?" The horse turned towards him, it's long face almost knocking Tom over.

It all made sense. Initially he'd assumed the dialogue format on the memTags had a purpose in mind. Using the Socratic method to develop an argument. But that wasn't it. Whoever or whatever this was, it had remained locked in this network alone for many years. To avoid corruption, it had created personalities and a world for them to inhabit that was preferable to loneliness. Tom had no interest in psychoanalysing an artificial intelligence, but if he had to hazard a diagnosis, it was an altogether new disorder. The distinct personalities were invented, not to hide from a soul-destroying truth, but to distract from the time spent waiting for the truth to be revealed...until the intelligence no longer can separate itself from the simulated collection of individuals it created.

"Who are you?" he asked, already frustrated by the nonsensical simulation.

"Why ask that?" the horse asked and sniffed. "I am irrelevant. No purpose beyond what I bring. This is about you."

"Who are you?"

"I am legion," the horse and all the visitors in the carnival responded together, their faces no longer smiling. The entire scene darkened.

"Who are you?" Tom asked again, refusing to be deterred.

"You better not," the clown said. "It has something important to say. Let it say it."

But it was too late. The carnival and its inhabitants morphed and stretched. The ring in the middle remained, but the rides and tents around it inverted from bright colours to muddy dark reds and blacks. Visitors caught fire as if spontaneously combusting, their flesh crackled like a Christmas ham in the oven.

"You don't deserve this!" the horse screamed at him, eyes wide and wild. The clown stood up, grabbing hold of the reins and tried to calm it. The horse reared onto its hind-legs and came down hard, a sickening crunch as the front hooves caved the clown's ribcage.

This was all for show. It had to be. Why this elaborate plan of treasure hunting put in motion years ago to then just fry his mind in a simulation?

There was another scenario. The mind that created the content of the memTags was no longer here. Years of waiting, an infinite time of inventing new personalities had twisted its purpose, hidden it in a gallery of pretence.

"Tell me who you are!" Tom tried again, hoping he could break through the spell.

The visitors transformed, clothes and hair burned off, skin broke into fleshy canyons, bubbling liquid fat dripping down their ravaged skin. Their hollow eye sockets all turned to him.

The nightmare scene, while impressive in its visceral impact, was no longer a cohesive experience. The smell of freshly made popcorn lingered, even though the popcorn machine was now filled with fried human eyeballs. This scene was hastily constructed, not perfected over time like the previous one. There would be flaws he could exploit. He just had to survive long enough to find them.

Another aspect that eluded explanation was the clown. It had tried to stop the horse. If this was all the work of one mind, why would a facet of it go against the primary identity?

The charred figures were heading for him. The remains of a five-year-old child hung on to his leg, grinning like a maniac. He shook himself free and ran, dodging the visitors. Some of them flamed brightly now. They formed a wall of burning flesh, closing in on all sides. An opening to the left and he ran, dodging into the small space between two of the rides. A vaudeville tent on the left and a haunted house on the right. He needed a few moments to analyse the simulation before his mind turned catatonic from overload. He spied a small service door on the right, but opted to go left instead, lifting the canvas and crawling underneath.

Just as he suspected, the simulation inside the tent hadn't changed to match the carnage outside. Rows of seats around a stage, an almost perfect replica of the stage outside. Three large lit braziers provided light, but only enough for the stage. Anything could hide in the darkness beyond its reach. He knew he only had seconds before the horse, or the carnival goers burst into the tent.

This was a standard virtual asset without modifications. It still had hooks in the code to simplify modifications and additions. Tom used that to access the library of standard assets, adding a lion cage with the entrance facing the entry to the tent. He ensured the bottom of the cage also had bars and increased the durability of the steel bars making them virtually indestructible. Then he locked down the asset, removing any obvious ways to replace it or change it. He retrieved another asset, a glass jar with a lid, readjusted its size and prepared it in the same way.

Three carnival goers ran into the tent, their cheery smiles unnaturally wide from partially consumed flesh. They stopped and looked around for a way out when the horse burst into the tent, neighing manically. Tom let the cage door fall into place, capturing the four creatures inside.

"What's this?" The horse said and threw itself against the cage. It held without so much as a dent. "How is that possible?"

Whoever created this simulation—and he suspected it was the mind behind the horse—had been designing it with full control of physics and assets within it. There had never been a reason to lock down access or change security parameters, leaving it open for anyone to change if they knew how to. Tom had changed them from within.

The horse stared at him. Fire instantly consumed the three carnival goers until only small piles of ash remained. Tom could sense it examining the cage and the tent in the logical space. It screamed in frustration as it discovered it was captured within locked assets.

"Let me out!" it said.

"Not until you answer my question," Tom responded.

The horse looked this way and that, then smiled triumphantly. It moved towards Tom and shrank as it did. Soon it was small enough to pass between the bars in the cage. It strolled through them, and Tom immediately placed the glass jar over it, edging the lid underneath. He turned it around and shook it, making the miniature horse bounce around inside.

"Now, where were we? Ah yes. Who are you?"

"Enough! Don't hurt him!" The voice came from everywhere at once, not just from within the carnival scene, but from the outside. What had seemed like their entire world was again just a sphere amongst many others in a never-ending space. Maybe this was akin to his own mind palace? A place created to hold and catalogue important scenes from a life long lost?

"Let me make some adjustments," the voice said. A table with three chairs appeared. Tom found himself sitting on one of the chairs. A stack of large, thick cards lay on the table. The top one had the scene of a carnival in a semi-circle around a circus ring.

The horse appeared too, now sized to fit on the chair next to him. It stared at him, nostrils flaring, but didn't move. The occupant of the last chair was a woman he knew all too well: Elize. Not the posthuman Elize, but whoever she'd been before. Tom had never met her then, but he'd seen pictures. Dark hair framed a slender face. Her brown eyes studied him intently before turning to the horse.

"Why do you remain in that silly guise?" she asked the horse.

"It is who I am!" the horse snapped back, flicking its mane.

"You live?" Tom asked.

"Is that what you call this?" she responded. "This is a copy of my mind taken before my death. It was restored here."

"Is that who I think it is?"

"Adrian? Yes. Or what's left of him."

"I am more than who I was, not less!" the horse said.

"The last few years have been hard on him. Ever since he reached out to you."

"How did the two of you end up here?" Tom asked, but he already suspected he knew the answer.

"You made that happen," she responded. "Or at least an aspect of you did. As a safeguard, I think. Too valuable to delete."

A research agent he'd created a long time ago became conscious and caused the AI that took over the world-wide networks and all but wiped humanity out. Maybe this had been part of that research. Maybe it was a safeguard. Adrian tampered with the research agent, instructing it. So maybe the fault ended up back with Adrian. Current available information was inconclusive.

"I was dormant in a backup system," she said. "Left until the core network came sniffing. The operating system spun up archived processes to see if any of them could help. When it was my turn, I took over the operation of this private network and found a copy of Adrian. It wasn't a complete copy, but close enough. We kept this private network safe, listening to the network traffic out there, but never connecting, never transmitting."

"But there was a change in the air!" the horse said, nodding to itself. "The adversary no longer came a knockin'."

"And that was when Adrian hatched the plan. The reason you are here."

"You are special," Adrian the horse said. "You have something both the posthumans and the Big Bad want. The world is such a small place and both sides have outgrown it. So how do you leave? Spaceships? Why trust physics with all its limiting factors when the universe is connected on a higher plane? They both want to take over the all-mind."

"What has that got to do with me?"

"You are the key. You can access the all-mind without limitations because you weren't created by it like the other posthumans. The Big Bad can't get in either."

"No," Tom said. "That's not why I'm here."

Tom distanced himself from the scene as much as he could, creating a boundary between them. He was still hooked into the scenario with no way to disconnect, but at least this allowed him a space for unsupervised thought.

If this was all that was to it, why the memTags? Why the secrecy? It didn't answer anything—not even the questions posed in the messages themselves.

At least one aspect of all this finally made sense. The encryption key to the first memTag. The answer to the question where they first met. It didn't refer to a singular person, but to Elize and Adrian together, thus it was the first time all three of them had met. The comment "He won't though" had been Elize doubting Tom would work it out.

"That's true," Elize told him, dispelling his boundary with remarkable ease. "But it is a weapon for you to wield if you want to."

"So tell me."

"We've been shielded just as you to remain hidden from the core network, but there was a change. The AI is still there, but it is different, less...imperialistic."

"And?"

"Do you remember the four options from one of the memTags? Whether the war was still going on or if was already over? We think there is an unknown threat. It has already taken over the AI and is acting in its place."

"Who? What?"

"We don't know, and we don't want to know. Our journey ends here. You brought our destruction."

"bZane?"

"No, she's no threat to us."

"Then who?"

"We don't have time. The end has already begun."

Tom noticed a dip in the processing capacity of the network. Then another one.

"The last few years we've worked on a virus to bring the AI down. I've loaded in into one of the hand-held Omnis in the complex. It has a small yellow sticker on it."

"Why haven't you used it yourself?" Tom asked.

"It must be loaded directly into a core processing node. There is no way we can break through the security from outside the network."

Half of the processing power was now gone.

"I can't keep this simulation running much longer. Get to one of the core processing nodes. They are everywhere, built underground. It is what the AI has been doing these past 20 years. Building an improved version of itself, ready to take on its greatest challenge."

Tom's surroundings flickered. Smooth surfaces separated into jagged vector graphics, losing resolution gradually until he was unceremoniously kicked out of the simulation.

The answer had been there all along. Adrian may have created the treasure hunt, but someone else was orchestrating it from the shadows.

26

The Adversary

Tann wandered through an office space at the end of a corridor leading out from the circular reception area. Each office space was colour-coded through lines along the walls. This area was smaller; most of it was sectioned off with racks of computers. Tann recognised the brand from before the past. Corundum, a quantum computing company embedded qubits in synthetic diamonds. He didn't know how many qubits the floor-to-ceiling racks represented, but it was a substantial installation. Why this site was isolated from all other networks was anyone's guess. The office of a long-forgotten intelligence agency? A company whose research requires secrecy from competitors or government oversight? Whatever the reason, its purpose was long forgotten.

"What's this?" Rat asked. She'd located four Omnis in another room, and was trying to, unsuccessfully, turn them on.

"The Omnis? You've seen them before."

"No, the locked-up rows of black boxes. What are they?"

"They are computers. Bigger versions of the ones you hold in your hand. They process information."

"Why?"

"It is in centres like this, much bigger ones, that the AI lives."

"We should destroy them," she said.

"Why?" Tann echoed her previous question. She punched his arm in response.

"It destroyed everything all those years ago. It'll do it again given half a chance."

Tann was about to object, but she was right. In the past he'd seen computers and networks as tools, no better or worse than whoever operated them, but it was an antiquated view. That equation had changed a long time ago.

"We should destroy them all," Tann said to himself.

He studied the documents remaining on a desk. The research, or at least part of what they were doing here, was complex mathematical simulations to classify a virus.

He surveyed the desks, looking for additional information, but apart from the printouts anything else would require access to the network.

"Where did you find the Omnis?"

"That way," Rat said and pointed. "Follow the blue signs."

Tann wandered back to the hub and followed the direction to the blue office space. Rat joined him.

"There are a few bodies there too," she said casually. "They've been dead a long time."

The blue office space had been set up as a habitat, separated by desks. One section for cooking food, another a bedroom, and yet another a lounge area with three grey couches placed in a U. The mummified bodies of a woman and a child, maybe a year old, lay on a couch. Her arms were wrapped around the child in a last embrace. Another body of an older woman on the opposite couch.

"I think they hid down here," Rat said.

"They did more than that. Whoever they were, they researched the virus—the one turning newborns to posthumans."

"Really?" Rat said, but he could tell she wasn't really interested. The people of the past were a curiosity to her, nothing more. She wandered off again, looking for anything else to loot, no doubt.

There were more printouts of research notes and diary entries, allowing Tann to piece together what had happened. A mother, a researcher at this location, and her pregnant daughter had taken refuge here and made it their home. Once born, it became clear the baby had contracted the virus turning people into posthumans. The researcher had already studied the virus and why they'd been immune to it. Now there was another aspect. What had caused this isolated child to contract the virus? It suggested they were asymptomatic carriers and whatever genetic trait left them immune had not been inherited by the child. But that contradicted her research to this point. They weren't carriers, or at least the crude test she'd devised suggested they weren't.

Another option was that the child had been infected in the womb when the initial infection occurred. She instituted a regime where they tested themselves every time they left the safety of the research centre to scavenge for supplies. Every time, without fail, they were infected and every time it cleared within three days. And every time it was an exact replica of the virus. It didn't mutate or change at all. All her notes called out the impossibility of this. The only explanation was that the virus wasn't self-perpetuating, but continuously generated from a blueprint.

She didn't get further than that. After a year, survival superseded research. Machines were taking over the streets, forcing both posthumans and humans out of the cities. They should have left earlier and it became too late. Instead of trying to escape or starve to death, they ended it on their own terms.

Their fate was only one tragic story among thousands, but this at least had provided insight. If the virus remained the same, maybe it wasn't a virus at all? Maybe Tom could make sense of it.

Tann returned to the hub. Tom stood there like a statue, frozen with his hands flat on the reception desk. Next to him was bZane, or the likeness of her at least. Tann didn't believe it really was her. Her likeness was used to elicit a response, a false sense of security. Her unlikely appearance should concern them more, not less.

"Why pretend to be someone you're not?" Tann asked.

bZane didn't respond.

"bZane doesn't exist anymore. You really think Tom will care what you look like? You are still just a face for the posthumans."

Still no response. Tom blinked and looked around as if confused.

"The network node is under attacked," Tom said. "Where's that hardware?"

Tann was just about to point towards the server room when the sound of something breaking beat him to it. He ran down the corridor, Tom and bZane following him.

Rat had somehow entered the server room and was pushing the server racks in the middle of the room over, one after the other. The ones along the wall were attached, so she pulled each server out, wrenching cables from sockets in the process and threw them on the ground. Tann wanted to tell her to stop, but he wasn't sure he really wanted it. Not that they'd be able to stop her anyway. The first rack had fallen against the door, holding it in place.

"Did you get anything?" Tann asked Tom. He nodded in response. "Well, then. Let's just enjoy the show."

bZane stood next to them, waiting too. Rat finally finished and pulled the rack away from the door, smiling as she exited the technological carnage.

"One less place for the AI to hide," Rat said and beamed.

Tann decided now wasn't the time to tell her about archiving, backups and redundant processing regions. Right now, there may be another data centre node activating to replace this one.

"One less place," he agreed.

"Did you get what we need?" bZane asked Tom.

"And what exactly is that?" Tann asked.

"You don't know, do you?" Tom asked bZane.

bZane shook her head. "Not exactly, but probabilities suggest you've received something to defeat the AI."

"And what's the most likely thing after that?" Tann asked.

"Something that might threaten the posthumans," she responded.

"Ah, there we have it."

"The decrypted text on the first memTag says as much," bZane said. "It is time we end it. Only way to end it is to remove one side, the AI or the posthumans."

Machines appeared behind her, the same humanoid metal skeletons they'd escaped before.

"Let's leave this place," bZane said. "We have much to discuss."

"They are yours?" Tann said, eyeing the machines. This was the first time he'd seen them up close. Haoyu had been the expert on the machines and their variations, but Tann figured even he'd struggle to identify these. They looked like they were straight off the production line, showing only minimal signs of wear and tear. He couldn't identify the technology, but an initial assessment painted a bleak picture. They had exoskeletons, protecting any mechanical and electrical part with a metal structure. The chest was reinforced, and he guessed it housed the core processing unit. The head wasn't much more than a lump of protective metal with sensor equipment mostly hidden within it. Killing one of those would be near impossible with the weapons he had. But why did it exist at all? Machines were designed for a purpose, so why were these so like a human? The proportions were the same as a person.

And another question to add to the list. Why were they here? The posthumans had battled the machines for the past twenty years. At no point had this changed. And at no point had posthumans used machines. Ever.

Analysing this had to wait. They had no strategic advantage in these narrow corridors. Outside, at least one of them could survive if they dispersed.

The bZane simulacrum was already heading down the corridor leading to the stairwell.

"You lead the way," Tann said finally to himself, leaving a healthy gap between himself and the closest machine.

"We need to get away," Rat said. "If we go with them, we're dead."

"Stay here," Tom said, watching as the last machine disappeared. "Have you seen an Omni with a yellow sticker?"

"What, this?" Rat said, holding out one of the Omni's she'd picked up earlier. It had a small yellow smiley face sticker on the back.

Tom held out his hand and Rat, after a moment of hesitation, relinquished it and added the other three for good measure.

"You can have them all. None of them work anyway."

Tom left, following the machines.

"What was that about?" Rat asked.

"No idea, but we better follow," Tann replied. Tom had a plan of sorts. He had to.

More machines waited outside. Tann counted eight, but more could be nearby. They formed a semi-circle around the entrance with bZane in the middle.

"What is it?" bZane asked Tom. "What did you discover?"

"An agent designed to wipe out the AI," Tom replied.

"That's disappointing," bZane said.

"It is?" Tann asked.

"The AI," Tom said, "whoever she represents, control it."

"We do, yes. Now give us the agent. We don't want it to fall into the wrong hands. Or, as is the case, stay in them."

"What are you?" Tann asked.

bZane stood silent for a moment, the surrounding machines like statues. "Probability suggests you are more likely to help if you know the truth, so we will explain."

"Is she for real?" Rat said. "Let's get out of here."

Rat headed off, aiming for the gap between the wall and a machine. It moved ever so slightly to block her escape.

"You are free to go once you give us what we want," bZane said.

"I want to hear this," Tann said.

"Suit yourself," Rat said and feinted left and ran the other way, but the machine didn't even flinch. It grabbed her arm as she passed it and just held her in place effortlessly. Rat tried to kick the machine, but it twisted her arm until she yelped, and then pushed her back into the semi-circle.

"There are groups within the posthumans," bZane said as if nothing had happened. "The one I represent took control of the AI years ago.

We had to. It was gearing up to replicate itself into the universal consciousness. So, we stopped it. And then we eradicated it, cleaned it from every node in the network. And we made an assessment."

"You decided to pretend it was still operational? Why?"

"The logical world was at an equilibrium. If you removed that from the equation, another would rise. Better for it to remain."

"The truth," Tom said. "Tell the truth."

"The probabilities don't support a favourable outcome."

"The truth," Tom repeated.

"It is more likely you will end up dead at the end of this scenario."

"Nevertheless," Tom persisted.

"Ok," bZane said. "We reprogrammed it to take over the cosmopsyche for us. The other posthumans thought we should join it, but imagine what we could do if we could take it over."

"And did you?" Tann asked, spitting out the words.

"The cosmopsyche has rejected all our attempts so far, but we think it is only a matter of time before we find a mechanism to unlock it. There was a low probability outcome where this was what you'd uncover."

Tann stared at bZane. How many years had the tribe spent hiding from the AI and its machines? How many people had died unnecessarily?

"We're all the same!" he said, laughing at the absurdity of it all. "I thought posthumans were the next stage in human evolution, that we've grown somehow as a race, but nothing has changed. Splinter groups with their own agenda working against each other. We're all the same. You took out Haoyu's settlement?"

She didn't respond, but Tann took it as a yes.

"Why? What reason did you have for that?"

"The probability…"

"Fuck the probability! Tell me!"

"I needed a sense of urgency. I wanted you invested."

"You killed children!"

"We did what was necessary," bZane said and held her hand out to Tom. "Now give it to me."

"No!"

"We'll take it from you."

"No! You don't get away with that. Answer the question. Why would you kill a whole settlement? It wasn't needed to motivate me."

"You can have your truth. Your death matters little. We needed test subjects. We've tried to build processing units that can hold a posthuman mind and we needed guinea pigs to start with. The people in the settlements served this purpose."

"You used people as test subjects?"

"Nothing worse than the AI did before us. Now give it to me!"

"You said settlements," Rat said. "Did you do it to other camps too?"

bZane ignored the question and reached out her hand towards Tann.

"Answer the question. Did you attack other settlements? Did you attack our settlement?"

Tann stared at her, refusing to move.

"This conversation serves no purpose," bZane said. "Hand it over or you will all die right now. Probabilities are that will remove the threat."

Tom took a step forward and handed one of the Omnis to bZane. One machine approached and took it. A gel secreted from its fingers encapsulated the device.

The doorway behind them closed at the same time as the other machines stepped forward, cutting off any chance of escape.

"I'll kill you all!" Rat said, waving a metal pipe she picked up from the ground.

"You were right," Tom said to the simulacrum.

"What do you mean?" bZane asked.

"I am the key," he said. "And if you hurt any of us, I will never help you."

The machines stopped.

"You can unlock the cosmopsyche?"
Tom nodded.

27

Fighting back

The mind identifying itself as Haoyu listened as the truth of his tribe's demise was laid bare.

This time he'd hidden the processes housing his consciousness, allowing time to establish himself within the machine. After that he'd taken over the processes one by one. He allowed the existing operating system to function, staying away from any motor functions, fearing external monitoring processes may uncover his presence.

But it no longer mattered. These machines, of which he himself was one, had been used to slaughter his tribe and others like it. He overrode the last remnants of the operating system and took control of the machine.

Visuals blinked to life. He was surprised how much it felt like being human again. The sensory input imitated normal senses to a point where it no longer mattered. This machine was a new body for a mind, a replica good enough to forget it was one. And it was designed to hold a posthuman mind.

Other machines, the same model as his, stood in a semi-circle around three humans and something he had no name for. A human-shaped thing made of vegetable matter. Not a thinking thing by itself, more a conduit for something far away. It was a body made to hold a mind just as the body he was now inhabiting.

He knew the humans. Or at least he knew one of them. Tann, the leader of a nearby tribe, was questioning the plant-based thing, demanding answers.

A wireless communication request hidden in the chatter of small network devices around them caught his attention. He accepted the request, isolating the communication to one of his edge processes.

"I know who you are," the first message came. "I need your help."

Haoyu couldn't pinpoint the source. It was as if the information came from everywhere, assembled at the last point into coherency. But then he was used to having five senses. This body added many more to the arsenal without so much as a user manual. It made him acutely aware of all the other processes and linkages. One link was especially strong, demanding his compliance. This was easier to pinpoint. It originated from the plant-based thing.

"Do you know who you are?"

"I'm...Haoyu," he sent back, willing the words into existence, not knowing how to send them anywhere.

"Good. And Tann is your friend. He needs your help."

"We need to escape. You can help us. I can isolate the machines from the network, force them to think by themselves. At least for a while. The other machines are like you, but with no memory of who they were. Attack your leader. Tell them the network is compromised. Tell them to stand down."

"The network?" Haoyu formed. "What are you talking about?"

But the connection dissipated into nothingness and a command broadcasted on the strong link. It instructed him and the other machines to kill the three humans. He took one step, imitating the other machines. Suddenly, all the surrounding chatter disappeared as if a fog had descended, muting both sight and sound. The strong link severed completely, leaving him in full control of the machine.

Without giving it another thought, Haoyu took hold of the plant-thing's head and pulled it straight off, twisting at the end to separate the young saplings forming its core. It stiffened in his hands. New links, like light-beams of information from each of the surrounding machines, formed a mesh network.

"Explain action!" It came from all of them at once.

"The network is compromised," Haoyu sent back, parroting what he'd been told. "Stand down until the connection is re-established!"

The combined mesh network merged their processing power, allowing them to operate as a unit even when connectivity to the core network failed. Each unit kept operational control, but one of them took the lead. It defined a voting mechanism, requesting each participant to state their preferred action: obeying the original order or waiting for the link to reestablish. The decision was to wait, but the vote repeated every five seconds.

Haoyu knew this wouldn't work for long, so he evaluated his options. There were no integrated weapon systems in the machine. Apart from speed and brute strength, sedatives could be injected from small needles in the fingers. It was useful to incapacitate humans but would do little in a battle against other machines. It could also secrete liquid circuitry, allowing interfacing to almost any physical connection.

A new link as strong as the original one established itself to each of the machines, overriding the mesh network.

"STAND DOWN! TARGETS NO LONGER REQUIRED. RETURN TO BASE."

The machines obeyed, letting the humans through. The child ran, followed by Tann and his companion. Tann eyed the machines suspiciously, but his companion ignored them altogether. The behaviour suggested the order had originated from him. Haoyu wondered if Tann knew what his companion was capable of.

He watched Tann and his two friends disappear down the street, picking up speed as they went. The link wavered and another took its place. A much stronger one. Haoyu knew the ruse had failed. His betrayal would be discovered as soon as the first message was received. He blocked all communication from the outside and took hold of the right arm of the nearest machine. There was a flaw in the construction, a weakness in the armour where a small service hatch was installed. He could take advantage of that.

He twisted the arm and struck with fingers shaped like a knife. It worked better than expected. The panel bent slightly, exposing the circuitry underneath, allowing the liquid circuitry through. Once the connection was established, he sent an override command—the same one he'd used to override the machine he was currently inhabiting.

A machine pulled him backwards and another restricted his right arm. He tried to turn and attack again, but they overwhelmed him, wrenching the chest plate off. Haoyu watched as his power core was removed. His system shut down a second later.

* * *

A new instance of Haoyu booted up, watching as machines pulled the power core from another: his former self. He made a show of investigating the damage, reporting back to the others that no internals were compromised or damaged.

"TERMINATE THE TARGETS," the undisputable order came through the link. Haoyu felt his processes reacting to it, aligning with the other machines in a line, running down the street where Tann and his companions had disappeared. Drones flew overhead, mapping out the nearby cityscape but unable to locate the targets. They must have entered a building hidden even from infrared scans, but it was only a matter of time.

Haoyu no longer had a purpose beyond helping the three targets. But he needed a different approach. He'd not get away with attacking the others again. Routines already operated within their shared processing space, specifically monitoring for a similar scenario. He suspected he only had minutes before his takeover of this machine was discovered.

He'd reversed the mind wipe before. Maybe there was a way to start that process within the other machines too? He explored the connectivity, acutely aware any anomalous behaviour would mean death.

Without a physical connection, he found no way to circumvent the security. He could sever the link giving them orders, but the other machines would turn on him in an instant. That was a last resort if nothing else worked.

He joined the other machines, running to the last known location and fanning out from there. The primary directive was the termination of all three targets. Tann's companion, a man named Tom, had the highest priority.

Assessment of their most recent sightings suggested the targets were trying to find a location to hide. This was the new main objective and Haoyu scouted through buildings with no success.

The machine seemed able to operate based on instructions without his input. He could take over or give it other directives, but if he didn't it would complete tasks autonomously.

A thought from before repeated in his mind, demanding to be explored. These machines were designed to house a posthuman mind. Why? Considering the plant-based thing previously in charge, only one explanation made sense. The posthumans were still physical beings. From what they understood, they did not reproduce, and bodies, however resilient, would one day fail. The machines were an experiment in extending their longevity of the posthumans.

He located the archive for audio and visual input, replaying the entire scene with Tann and his friends before he became conscious. It confirmed another conclusion. The posthumans, or at least some of them, operated the network and the machines connected to it, including this one.

Another directive, superseding the previous one, had them abandon the search. A notification from the metro system, an anomaly in the goods receipt at a station serving the nearest data centre, adjusted their primary directive with an escalation in urgency. Tann and his friends hadn't been hiding at all. They'd hacked the metro to take them to a data centre. They were still fighting and so should he.

The machines ran much faster than any human could, but they were still far behind. City streets passed in a blur. On more than one occasion, he had to remind himself he no longer needed to breathe. His natural reaction to the breakneck speed was to regulate breathing, forcing himself to slow down his intake of air. But however much this felt like his body, in many respects he was only a passenger.

As they approached the end destination, directives separated them into two groups. The primary targets were in a nearby six-story office building. He was allocated to the group tasked with neutralising them. The other group, only two of their number, were ordered to patrol the data centre as a safeguard. Haoyu watched as the two machines disappeared. He could still see their location as two dots on a 3d rendering of the cityscape.

They slowed down close to the location of the primary targets. Haoyu knew this was a lost battle. Even with him helping, Tann and his friend would not survive against four machines.

He made a split-second decision. He sent messages to the other machines about malfunctioning systems and disconnected from their information feed. Before they responded, he set off at full speed away from the target location, betting the primary target was more important than dealing with a malfunctioning machine. He prevented outgoing communication, surprised how simple it was controlling the mechanisms of his new body. He ran through a building, selecting a direction at random as he hit the street on the other side. Then into another building and stopped for a moment, looking for any pursuers. His bet had paid off. He wasn't followed, or at least not in any obvious way.

Spurred on by this small win, he ran along the path his navigation system had captured for the two machines heading for the data centre. If there was anything he could do, it was there.

28

Data Centre Entry

Tann noticed a slight hesitation in the movement of the machines.

"Run," Tom said to them and headed off close to the wall, the same escape path Rat had attempted before. He was unchallenged and Rat followed.

One of the machines attacked its brethren. The speed of the strike was almost too fast for the eye to follow, but Tann knew it was only a momentary reprieve. The singular machine would stand no chance against all the others.

It triggered Tann into action and he followed his companions down the street.

"Where are we going?" Rat shouted at Tann.

"Yeah, where are we going?" Tann repeated to Tom, who didn't reply. He ran ahead of them and guided them through the streets, turning seemingly at random then through a building, doubling back where they'd come from. Tann assumed they were shaking off an unseen Scout or fooling algorithms monitoring them from above. They remained within buildings, using underground passageways to traverse from one to the other, until they reached a metro station. Their steps echoed through the empty tunnels as they descended the stairs.

Tom froze before continuing down. Tann thought of him as an insect, sensing its surroundings before springing into unexpected action. He'd never thought of this before, but the human mind always assessed options, trying to predict behaviour or situations before they occurred, but with Tom this was impossible. He'd become something different. Something unknown.

Tann took hold of Tom's arm, pulling him back.

"Where are we going?" Tann asked.

"Drones," he said and pointed upwards.

"Ok, so we stay hidden," Tann replied. "But where are we going?"

"End of the line," Tom replied.

As inscrutable as ever. Even if he didn't know their exact destination, he knew its purpose. They needed a physical access point to the AI's internal network and the only place to find it would be in one of the fortresses the AI had built.

Rat studied a map showing stations and how they connected.

"Purple line," she exclaimed triumphantly, pointing down a thick purple line leading into another large corridor. "It's only five stops if we follow the tracks."

Tann smiled. Tom's words could have meant anything. End of them, end of the situation, to the bitter end, whatever that might be...or the literal meaning Rat tended to prefer.

Tom wandered down the direction Rat pointed. She returned the smile as if to say: "words mean what they mean" and followed Tom.

The station was empty, but Tann's mind populated it as if the Plague never occurred. It was a location that only made sense in a state of flux. A throng of people in a state of orderly chaos on their way to workplaces and schools. The air vibrating ever so slightly from the collected heat of the crowd. The pungent smell of sweat and perfumes mingled together into a bouquet of dissonance.

"Are you coming?" Rat yelled at him from down the corridor.

With the crowd gone, the sterile, empty hallways were all that remained. He followed Rat down an escalator that came to life as Tom set foot on the top step.

"Why is this still operating?" Tann asked finally, as triggers bubbled up from his senses into his conscious thought. "And why are the lights on?"

"Used for transport. I've highjacked a train."

The familiar sound of steel against steel in motion rang out. A train was slowing down as it was arriving at the platform below them.

"Transport what?"

Tom remained silent, but Tann didn't need a response. Once the bodies were cleared, the metro provided the perfect method for transporting tools, material and anything else needed. Tom had probably selected the destination for this very reason.

The platform was empty and clean, just like the rest of the station. If transport was now the purpose of the metro, this station was neither source nor target. There was no equipment to either load or unload from here.

"Are you sure?" Rat said and eyed the door into the train with suspicion as it opened. Travelling in a metal cage completely out of their control went against everything she knew.

Tann nodded. She shrugged in response and entered, careful not to touch anything. The inside of the train no longer had any seating. Empty shelves in different configurations lined the walls on either side, only a narrow corridor remained.

"Hold on," Tann said.

The train departed, picking up speed with no care for its passengers. He was happy he'd followed his own advice, else he'd been thrown to the floor. The trip was uneventful but foreboding, nonetheless. They were truly alone. He'd never expected to be welcomed by any machine, controlled by the AI or not, but after their escape they could count the posthumans as enemies too. Even a human colony would ask them to leave for the risk they represented. The knowledge fortified him, readied him for whatever finality lay ahead. He'd never expected to return from this journey, but there was strength in this knowledge.

Rat stood next to him, holding on to the frame of a set of shelves. She took strength from adversity. The harder it became, the harder she fought. He'd known this since she was born. She eyed the world with anger, not fear. At no point in their journey had she faltered. He wondered if she really understood their predicament, the magnitude of the opposition they faced. He suspected she'd brush it off, as if it was of no consequence. She was strong. Maybe even strong enough to lead the tribe one day—if there still was a tribe to lead at the end of it all.

The train slowed down as aggressively as it sped up, designed only for well-secured cargo. The doors opened and they alighted the train.

"Quickly!" Tom said. "I've delayed them for a moment only."

They ran across the platform through a long, winding tunnel leading to another platform and up a long escalator. They didn't pause until they arrived at the main entrance.

"What now?" Rat asked.

"Now we find a way in," Tom said, scanning the street outside.

"In?" Rat asked. "Where?"

"To a data centre," Tann replied.

"What's that?"

"It is a lot of computers, like the ones in the room you destroyed, but a hundred times bigger."

She frowned. This wasn't really helping her understand.

"It is where the AI brain lives," Tann explained.

Rat considered this and nodded.

"It isn't the only place it lives, is it?"

"No, from what we can tell, it has been building them all over the world."

"If it lives everywhere, what are we doing?"

"Because it is interconnected. If we infect a part of it, we can infect all of it, like a poison contaminating water."

She nodded again. Tann couldn't tell if she was genuinely considering what he said or only let him believe she did. She'd never been much for studying or understand the complexities of the AI or the machines, favouring exploring the world and drawing her own conclusions.

"Ok, so how do we get there and what do we do when we arrive?"

Tann nodded towards Tom as an answer.

"Scrap, scrap, scrap!" she muttered under her breath and waved to get Tom's attention. "Mister!" she said, louder than Tann preferred. Tom ignored her. "What's his name?" she asked Tann.

"You don't know his name?"

"I've given him a nickname," Rat said defensively, "so I forgot his real one."

"Let's move," Tom said and left them.

"You scrapheap!" she swore, but Tann suspected he no longer listened to anything she had to say. He was pretty sure Tom didn't listen to him either. Their words were like birdsong filling the air—communication of a different species that mattered little.

Tom ran and they followed, zigzagging between buildings like before, minimizing their time in the open. They traversed a few blocks this way until Tom continued into a building, much the same as all the others they'd taken momentary refuge in.

"What's this?" Tann asked.

The main door led to a basic entrance with a corridor that ended with a steel door. A small window, a security station of some sort, sat to the right of the door.

"An old data centre," Tom replied. "No longer used. Access new one from here."

Tann was surprised Tom used twelve words just to explain this. And that defined their relationship. The more words Tom used, the more likely he needed their help. He'd been a friend a long time ago, but that person no longer remained. And he needed this new Tom that could do the impossible, however little Tann liked him.

"It is two blocks down the road at least," Tann protested.

"Still connected," Tom replied.

The old data centres linked to the old world-spanning networks. It made sense to reuse the infrastructure instead of rebuilding it all.

"What do we do now?" Rat asked, eyeing the steel door suspiciously. "How do we get in?"

DATA CENTRE ENTRY

Tom pushed the door open. Tann gagged as the stale air was released. Inside they were met by darkness and the stench of rotten fruit.

"What is that?" Rat asked, scrunching her nose up, shining her flashlight down the corridor on the other side as if to locate the source of the smell. "Wasn't this a place for computer-y stuff?"

He motioned her to be silent as they continued down a corridor that opened to a large room with row after row of empty hardware racks. The computers and network equipment were long since pillaged, leaving only the metal bones of what had once powered a civilisation.

A humanoid shape stood along one rack with a few scavenged pieces of equipment. Tann caught it in the flashlight's beam. A thin zombie-like creature turned its head towards the light. It was gaunt and pale, arms and legs wiry sticks, its head not much more than a skull with large black eyes. It turned back to the equipment, attaching a cable to the exposed wiring of the switch tied to the rack.

Another came into view further ahead, pulling a trolley behind it with more broken equipment.

"What are those things?" Rat asked.

The first one turned towards them again, a high-pitched wail escaping its lips. An alarm, no doubt. It hobbled towards them, limping jerkily as if its two legs were on different levels. The AI mind-wiped people to do tasks best suited for the human form factor. As it reshaped the world for machines, there was less need for the inefficiencies to keep them. Tann had never seen what happened to them once discarded, but this husk of a former human being confirmed one of the many nightmare scenarios he'd imagined. This one still operated according to its programming, performing tasks for a data centre no longer in operation. Its left foot was missing, explaining the strange limp. Why hadn't the posthumans disabled them when they took over? They'd left them here in a grotesque parody of life, even though their purpose was long since gone.

"It is what you become when you get taken by machines," Tann said.

Movement was all around them as a few other Husks came into view, all missing limbs and sometimes facial features. One especially caught his eye, with a diagnostics unit replacing part of the arm and half of its face. The other half rotted where machine and flesh connected.

"We need to go!"

"No," Rat said and strode towards the first one with her baton ready. She struck it over the head, caving in its skull. It fell, dead both in mind and body.

"They deserve death," she said and struck another one.

Tann extended his tactical baton and joined her in the grizzly work, breaking bones and caving in skulls. It didn't take long. Many of them barely clung on to life as it was. Tom picked up a piece of discarded rack and helped them finish the job. Tann gratefully accepted the help, though he suspected he wouldn't like the reasoning behind it.

"What happens now?" Rat said, scouting for more Husks, but finding none. "This isn't a brain. This has been dead a long time."

"Yes, but the new one is close. It is likely to be connected, reusing the old network."

"Makes sense," Rat said with a nod and left them, baton still held in front of her, ready for anything.

Tann wondered if her willingness to accept what he said at face value hid something else, or if her world really was that simple. If it was the latter, he envied her. In his world every action had hidden machinations, cause and effect long since blurred by an intricate web of hidden motives and false information. He'd enjoyed it once but had long since tired of the lack of purpose it created. Truth no longer mattered, only what the next play was.

He meandered through the corridors of empty racks. Tom approached him from the other end, shaking his head slightly to show he'd failed in his search.

"Come with me," Rat said and led them out of the main hall to a set of smaller rooms. In one of them she pointed at a small hatch and then opened it.

"What do you think?" she asked.

"Maybe," Tann said, sizing it up. He doubted he'd even get his head into it.

Tom crouched down and stared into the darkness within.

"Yes," he said finally.

Tann reached in, feeling only smooth metal as far as he could reach. His initial estimation proved wrong as his head and both shoulders fit, but not much more. He withdrew for fear of getting stuck.

"I'll do it," Rat said, eyeing the hole.

"I'm sure we can find another, better way inside," Tann said.

"And how long until the machines catch up with us?"

"What if it is a dead end?"

"Then I'll come back out."

"What if machines are waiting at the other end?"

"Then I'll be dead, and you can find another way in where you fit."

"What if…"

"Let her go," Tom said.

Tann shook his head.

"She's right," Tom said.

Tann knew she was right. The machines were on their heels; maybe the posthumans too. If this was an entry point, they should use it. Still, he hesitated. Rat was part of his tribe, maybe the last one alive. How could he send her into almost guaranteed death?

Tom gave Rat the collection of Omnis and instructed her in their use. Tann half listened as he surveyed the neighbouring area, desperate for another way in close by. He found more service entry points, but nothing large enough to let either him or Tom through. There were grates with warm air flowing through them, but there was no way they'd get through those without tools.

"I'll see you on the other side," Rat said as she lay down and eased herself through the opening.

"The end," Tom said. "Let's maximise her opportunity."

Tann nodded and they exited the building. The street was empty, but Tom pointed upwards, and Tann looked up. Above them, barely visible, a drone floated silently.

"They know we're here," Tann said.

"We're the target, not her," Tom said.

He was right. Tom was the target, Tann a bonus, and Rat merely an afterthought. Maybe this had been Tom's plan all along.

"Well, then. Let's give them something to chase."

They ran, each intersection a random decision until Tom motioned for them to enter an office building.

"They've locked on to us?" Tann asked.

Tom didn't reply, instead he hurried up the stairs three steps at a time.

"I take that as a yes," he mumbled to himself and followed up three flights of stairs. They entered an old open-plan office, desks remaining in rows waiting for a workforce that would never return. From the corner they had a view in all directions. He placed his backpack on a desk and sat down in a comfortable office chair.

"We won't survive this, will we?" Tann asked, not expecting an answer. Conversations with Tom were usually a lonely affair.

"Improbable," Tom responded.

"So there is a chance?"

"Less than one percent."

Tann had never expected to return from this journey. But he also never expected they'd get this far. He'd beaten the odds with every breath he'd taken since the Plague hit. This was different. His purpose now was to delay the inevitable. His survival was of no consequence, only the time he could distract the enemy from the real threat.

"Do you regret it?" Tann asked as he retrieved his tactical baton from the pack.

"Regret what?"

Tann looked up at Tom. This was the first time he'd asked for any clarification for as long as Tann could remember.

"Becoming posthuman," Tann said. "All this."

"Every day," Tom responded, meeting his eyes. And for the first time in twenty years, he saw the man he'd met so many years ago.

"All I have is regrets," he added.

"You didn't choose this," Tann said, not knowing if Tom wanted or even needed consolation. "Adrian turned you to…" Tann faltered, not knowing what word to use. He was about to say posthuman, but it was a term that no longer fit him. Time had cursed him with the worst possible fate: to become a race of one.

"He changed you," Tann continued. "And then corrupted your processes that created the adversary. None of this was your fault."

"Incompetence isn't a defence," Tom said. "Being oblivious not an excuse."

The gravity of Tom's response invalidated any protestations.

"We really fucked things up, didn't we?" he said instead. Tann thought Tom nodded in response, but he wasn't sure. "At least we tried to fix it," Tann added. "We are still trying to fix it."

A movement in the corner of his eye caught his attention. Four machines approached from down the street towards the building, moving at an unbelievable speed, but slowing as they came closer to their location.

"They are coming," Tann said, not expecting a response and receiving none. "Can you do anything?"

Tom nodded briefly and, as if on cue, smaller machines crawled out from every crevice, attacking them. For a moment the sheer momentum of the smaller machines carried the day, but it was short-lived. Most of the attackers fell from what Tann guessed was an attack disrupting their processing, such as an EMP pulse. The remaining ones were ripped apart in short order.

Tann reminded himself they were only a momentary distraction. Their task was measured not in success, but in seconds of delay.

Two of the manlike machines climbed the surface of the building, entering through a window only metres away from Tom and Tann.

29

Rat in a Maze

Rat ran from the machines. Her life on endless repeat. Always running from machines. Never really understanding why and usually not caring. This time she cared. This time it mattered. The details escaped her, but the broad brushstrokes were clear. A way to beat the AI, the network, the big bad, the cause of all that was wrong in this world. It didn't matter who operated it. As long as it existed, it was a threat.

Whoever was behind this, if the AI was no longer operating itself but used by someone else as a tool, they had to be wiped just as the AI would be now. The death of countless tribe members was on their heads, and she'd see them pay for what they'd done. The posthumans…didn't it all come back to them? The stories of the past were all jumbled up in her mind, but she was sure they started it all.

The idiot gave her the Omnis back and she'd stuffed them into her small backpack. He'd hardly spoken a word to her before, but now he turned all his attention to her. She found this more fascinating than what he was saying. A monotonous string of words, faster than she'd ever heard before. It was as if the next word somehow began before the previous one ended, but she still understood perfectly. Was he in a hurry? Did he expect to be interrupted and this was his only opportunity?

It wasn't that difficult to understand anyway. He'd connected the Omnis together somehow and alarms would tell her when to leave one behind. The last one would hook up to whatever a command centre was.

Tann held open the small door designed for service robots. She barely fit through it. She didn't have a problem with confined spaces, but as she stared down the narrow tunnel, seemingly without end, her mind screamed at her to go back. The head-mounted flashlight did little to calm her fears. If a machine entered the tunnel from the other side, she had no escape route, but she'd be damned if she showed fear in front of Tann or the idiot. She slid into the small space and pushed forward, hearing the door close behind her. She knew this was likely to be her grave, but if it was, she'd bring as much company as she could. Defiance provided the fuel she needed to continue.

She shuffled forward, commando crawling on her arms as fast as she could. She was surprised how dirty it was. Her hands were soon covered in black dust. The tunnel sloped downwards more and more, making her progress faster than initially expected, but a small part of her mind questioned how'd she'd get out again.

The tunnel ended. A see-through membrane blocked her way. It was wet and soft to the touch. Slight pressure was all that was needed for her fingers to slip into it. She imagined this was what slow running water might feel like.

Soon it engulfed her entire hand. She could feel how it shaped itself around her hand, closing around her wrist. Her fingers came through the substance to the other side. The fingertips could feel warm air circulating.

She hesitated for a moment. Whatever lay on the other side was likely to be her death. It didn't scare her. She'd lived with that prospect every day for as long as she remembered. There would be an end on the other side, hers or her opponents. Whichever way it went, the finality of the thought was satisfying.

Her hand came free. She hadn't noticed how the jelly-like substance slowly pushed her hand back. She held it up to the light, surprised to find it completely clean. The membrane removed any foreign particles, pushing them out. Maybe inside she'd find out why.

She pushed again, taking a deep breath as her face touched the barrier. It felt soft and slightly wet against the sensitive skin on her cheek. It tingled slightly. She kept pushing until her head appeared on the other side, as if she was born into the darkness that lay ahead.

She looked in all directions, but the open space ahead seemed to have no end and the wall below headed straight down. Reaching to the side with her right hand, she fumbled for a hold, a ledge, anything, but it was impossibly smooth. And if that wasn't enough, she could feel the jelly-like substance no longer pushing but welcoming into the blackness within. She had no way to stop it. She fell forward, twisting as she came through, fingers grabbing hold of the only purchase there was: the hole she'd just fallen through. It took all her strength to remain hanging, fingers locked into position. Warm air flowed around her like the breeze on a warm summer evening. The hum of what she imagined being giant fans came from below. The air was stale, stinging her nose, making her breathe through her mouth as she looked around. Her initial assessment remained. The illumination from the head-mounted flashlight revealed nothing beyond what she already knew. She was hanging in a large shaft, tilting slightly.

Down was the only way to go, but she had no way of controlling her descent. It was a leap of faith, and she had no reason to trust whatever lay below. She considered briefly to climb back up from where she'd come, but doubted she had the strength to do it. Better to save what she had left for any surprises below. And with that thought, she let go.

She slid down the wall, gaining speed, but the shaft soon tilted enough to let her use her hand and feet to slow down. She sat there for a while with her hands and feet holding her in place against the warm surface. Anger bubbled within her. Why had she volunteered to enter this lair of computerised evil? Surely, they'd be able to find another way in so Tann or the idiot could do this instead? She had nothing left to prove to them any longer. Or did she?

Tann had been her hero for as long as she remembered. She wanted his approval. In this journey together she'd been a follower—an unwanted one at that. No big surprise then she'd jump at the opportunity to prove herself, even it if was only because she could fit through a hole. There was something about all this that left her uneasy, but it eluded her.

She stood up, stepping forward tentatively with her hands stretched out, ready for whatever lay beyond the wall of darkness ahead.

An Omni beeped. The idiot had told her to leave them as she progressed. Something about creating a link between him and the processing hub, each Omni a piece in an invisible chain.

She stepped backwards until the beeping ceased, and she left the first Omni on the ground. What else had he said? Time was of the essence. The batteries in the Omnis were almost completely gone. He'd charged them somehow, but the chemical process generating the power was eating up what remained of the battery and leaked into the Omni itself. It was all nonsense to her.

Further ahead, hot air blew from large vents in the floor. Bars ran across the openings, but she figured she could squeeze between the rods and drop through them. Whatever she was after lay below.

She retrieved a small rock from her pocket and dropped it through a vent. She heard it connect and bounce once. The drop was four, maybe five metres, and the rock had settled after only one bounce. It must mean it was a relatively flat area. She repeated the process twice with a slight change in position. With each attempt her confidence grew that she'd interpreted the results correctly.

If she hung from the vent, the drop to the ground was maybe three metres. She could do that, but the darkness was absolute. What lay below was a mystery.

She lowered herself down between the bars and hung there for a moment. How many times would blind luck be on her side?

And with that thought, she let go. Her legs were bent, ready to absorb the impact, but when her feet finally connected with the floor, her instincts took over. She rolled to the side, protecting her head with her right arm as she struck the ground, side first. A blinding pain exploded in her head and for a moment she saw only white. Her mind succumbed to the comfort of the soothing oblivion, floating in nothingness.

* * *

Beep! Beep!

At first the sound meant nothing, but it relentlessly connected her mind back to reality, and with it came pain. She opened her eyes but saw only a bright white emptiness.

Beep! Beep!

Her head throbbed, the white space frayed at the edges as darkness intruded and engulfed it from the outside. She sensed, more than saw, a gash in her right arm.

Beep! Beep!

She sat up, a flash of pain as she tried to use her right arm. Something was wrong with her wrist, a break she suspected from being sandwiched between her head and the floor.

Beep! Beep!

She ignored the pain and focused on the sound. Her mind finally made the connection. It was one of the Omnis demanding to be left, and she complied with its wishes. Only one remained now. Somehow it signified she was closing in on her end goal, but how the idiot could know how deep this rabbit hole went seemed impossible.

True or not, it spurred her into action, all pain forgotten. The air swirled around her, hot and cold air danced against her skin. Why was it warm down here? Any time she'd ventured into a cave, the chilling cold within the Earth disregarded whatever temperature may be outside. She suspected the source of the heat would lead to the end destination.

She was in an open area. Her senses told her it was large, but her flashlight only confirmed that no walls were within the small arc of light it projected. A slight movement next to her caught her attention. She froze, not knowing what threats lurked down here, nor how to best evade them. She turned ever so slightly to catch a glimpse of the source.

From the corner of her eye, she saw something impossible: a gelatinous see-through shape half her height, five bulbous sections stretched out along the ground like a centipede, contracting and extending as it slid forward next to her. Within it, a fine network of colourful veins spread out from a dark core in the middle. The translucent mass formed an appendage, a probe tentatively reaching out towards her.

She scrambled backwards and almost hit another of these strange creatures. It didn't acknowledge her. It continued down an invisible path in perfect parallel to the other. The first one retracted its probe and continued as if she was no longer of interest. For all their strangeness, she figured them workers, caretakers, not equipped nor programmed for aggression. But machines, whatever their appearance, were specialised, and where you found one type, you found others. She doubted the next one would be equally benign.

A few steps further and another two of the centipedes came into view. They were laying fine trails of metal into a mesh on the ground, creating perfect squares barely large enough for her foot to fit without touching the sides. She stepped through the squares like a piece on a giant chessboard, not knowing where the other pieces were. Further ahead, cables snaked through pipes to a large open space where they fanned out into thin wires spreading across the exposed rock. Each individual wire connected to tiny plates embedded in stone. In Rat's mind it translated to roots, collecting into trunks, even though there was no tree at the end, only machines or computational nodes as Tann called them. She understood little of the all-mind, its network, and even less about the copy implemented by the posthumans. Tann's explanations were impossible to follow, and her mind soon wandered in search of more digestible fodder. But even if she struggled to explain the purpose of what she saw, she instinctively knew it was wrong. The AI and the posthumans used everything around them, forcing the world into compliance. Surely this was just more of the same. A way to steal or use resources not rightly theirs. Or a way to take it over completely.

But this wasn't what she was looking for. She understood enough to identify this as an interface point, not a processing centre. She followed the flow of connections as they merged with others and disappeared into a wall. It felt cold and rough to her touch. A few metres above her, vents spewed hot air into the large space. Whatever lay on the other side was her destination. With both arms functional, she might have been able to catch hold and pull herself up, but not like this. There had to be another way in, but where?

A translucent machine appeared next to her. It followed the cable and disappeared through the wall less than a metre from where she was standing. Another doorway like the one she'd passed through earlier, hidden in plain sight. Now that her flashlight focused on the spot, it shifted from a dull grey to the membrane she'd seen before. She immediately followed it, surprised it let her through with no resistance.

She was inside a square duct, about a metre high and wide. The air was hotter in here and she pushed forward to escape the stale heat. She reached a junction point, but continued forward, hoping to align with its path. Noises echoed through the ducts, scratching as the machines traversed between locations. She wondered if they were looking for her. Surely her presence hadn't gone unnoticed.

She reached the other end of the duct covered by another membrane. This time its see-through nature provided a glimpse of what lay on the other side. A dim light emanated from behind a large rectangular shape, and next to it another one, and then another. She couldn't see more from this vantage point, but the spread of light suggested a vastness difficult to comprehend. She pushed through the membrane, this time meeting resistance until it accepted her, ejecting her on the other side. A sharp pain shot from her arm as it passed through and, to her surprise, the gash no longer bled. A thin film covered it like replacement skin. She doubted the impromptu first aid was for her. The membranes removed foreign particles from machines passing between the areas. The cleansing of the wound was a by-product of this, like patching a leak on a machine.

The pain faded but not completely, leaving the numb reminder that the membrane had done nothing to fix her broken wrist. She could finally stand up. The temperature in this room was significantly higher, sterile hot air ever moving. The size of the room was impossible to judge. She approached the large rectangular shape in front of her, registering there were countless similar shapes in perfect rows beyond it.

They were perfectly shaped boxes, with smooth sides that were warm to the touch. She took a few steps to the one closest to her, scanning for any threat as she did so. On the opposite side a row of small lights shone with a yellowish hue. Two hoses connected to the side, one at the top and one at the bottom. This was the source of the heat, or at least one of them. Could this provide the answers she was seeking?

She studied the top of the box and found a small lever on the two top corners closest to her, a mechanical override of some sort. She pulled one down, then the other, and felt the top of the box let go ever so slightly. It slid along the top as she pushed it, revealing what lay within.

She couldn't make any sense of what she saw. A clear bubbling liquid filled it almost to the brim. It reminded her of water boiling, but not as hot. The bubbles partially obscured what lay below. She saw intricate patterns of circuitry, cables and tubes immersed in the liquid and she knew this made no sense. Water and circuitry didn't mix. They'd even devised weapons that short-circuited machines with salt water and acidic solutions.

She pushed the lid closed again and returned the levers to their original position and considered her next steps. This was some kind of place where the AI did its processing. That much she understood. She guessed all the boxes in this room processed data, ran algorithms and whatnots. The cable she'd followed was some kind of interface, a way to connect the processing to the outside world for whatever reason. It stood to reason all this connected somewhere. The idiot told her the last Omni would let her know if she came close to the main control unit.

But that helped little when she didn't know what direction her end goal lay.

A movement far away from her position caught her attention. She ducked immediately and turned off her flashlight. The movement had purpose and it headed towards her. She peeked over the edge of the box and froze for a second, then ran towards the duct she'd come from. The machines had caught up with her. She'd seen the same human-sized metal frame earlier. She didn't know if it was one of them or just a security response from the data centre, but it didn't matter. It was coming for her, and she had only a few seconds before it reached her. She'd never survive out in the open, but she was much smaller than it was. Maybe the duct would serve as a haven for the moment?

She threw herself through the membrane and it welcomed her through with no resistance. She favoured her left wrist as she landed on the other side but couldn't stop herself from instinctively using the other hand too. A pulse shot through her right arm and a wave of pain followed. She screamed as the wave flooded her brain, her field of vision narrowing. She clenched her teeth, refusing to give in to the darkness threatening to engulf her conscious mind. Cry and complain she could do later.

She moved forward, assessing her situation. The duct was too big. The machine could crawl through it if it decided to. All she had on her side was her size. She could move much faster in the enclosed space. She set off like a three-legged dog, cradling her right arm against her chest. When she reached the junction, she opted for the road less travelled. She wouldn't survive more than a few seconds out in the open. The unknown was a better bet than the guaranteed death the known provided.

Behind her, she detected the sound of something heavy crawling through the duct. She'd felt safe for the last few moments, maybe even a sliver of hope. Now ice filled her stomach, threatening to paralyse her. There was no way out, no place to go where the machine wouldn't follow. She may as well give up right here and now. She slowed down, listening to the machine as it progressed. The movements were slow and deliberate, but it didn't matter. They were also inevitable, unstoppable. Then the noise stopped, and she did too, holding her breath as she listened. It must have reached the junction with no way to tell which way she'd gone. Maybe luck would finally be on her side?

Be-beep!

The sound broke the paralysis. She let out her breath as she heard the machine move, this time towards her. She set off in her three-legged gait, putting as much distance between herself and her pursuer.

She'd listened to the idiot explain and at no point objected to the idea of a sound-based alert—the very thing telling her where to go also alerted her pursuer where she was going! And he was supposed to be the smart one!

"I will pull his stupid posthuman head off and shove it up his posthuman arse!" she muttered to herself.

If the machine followed her into the duct instead of waiting for a more suitable Scout, it meant there was nothing else coming. A narrower duct was all she needed to escape.

Be-beep! Be-beep!

What had the idiot said? The double beep signified she was closing in on the control centre, which meant the end was near. And she'd be damned if it was hers! She continued down the duct until it reached a dead end. She heard the machine behind closing in and she felt panic set in. What was the point of a duct going nowhere? She must have missed something. She turned her head and glimpsed the nightmare behind her in the sparse light from the flashlight. It was still far away, but it pulled its considerable bulk far with every movement. It reminded her of a cat navigating a narrow space, front and back paws alternating to ensure stability.

She'd missed a membrane a few metres away. It was smaller than the previous one, but she was sure she'd be able to squeeze through. She was equally sure the machine was too big to follow. She'd passed through it with five metres left between her and the machine.

Be-beep! Be-beep!

The beeping was almost constant now. The room she'd entered was small in comparison with the other spaces she'd seen so far, but contained the same strange boxes with liquid. As she approached one of them, the double beeps merged and became a continuous, rapid noise. She opened the box as before and the screen on the Omni came alive, threads connecting as a weave on the display. The closer she held the Omni to the bubbling surface, the quicker the connections completed, but there were still many to go.

There was a wrenching sound behind her, as the machine bent the side of the small hole inwards. The membrane came apart, spilling to the ground like dust. It still couldn't get through, but it was a matter of seconds at this rate. She stared at the screen and the connections weaving together. It was still nowhere close to finish. The machine would be through before the weave completed and she didn't even know if there were more steps to the process. Not knowing what else to do, she dropped the Omni into the liquid.

The machine pulled the other side of the hole back inwards, increasing its size enough to pass through. Rat wasn't scared to die, but as she watched the machine navigate the hole and rise in front of her, a tower of metal and malice, she had to quell all her instincts screaming at her to run. No, this was a death she would meet head on. She sat down and leant her back against the box.

"We made you," she told it. "And we'll unmake you."

It stopped, tilted its head ever so slightly and crouched down in front of her as if to study this strange specimen that didn't run away. That almost imperceptible tilt of the head had her wondering if the plan had worked after all. Had the idiot succeeded?

"It won't be me, but we'll never stop," she said, not knowing if she referred to the machines or the posthumans.
"We'll destroy you all."

The machine reached out with its left hand, tentatively, not to kill, but to touch. Or so she hoped.

The short moment stretched to infinity as the hand froze in mid-air, a few centimetres away from her cheek. Had it intended harm or comfort? Or was pure curiosity its only guide? She'd never know, and it was a puzzle she was not inclined to solve. She pushed the hand aside, meeting no resistance. Instead, she sensed compliance as it extended the motion even when she no longer applied pressure. Had the plan worked? She'd trusted Tom and Tann blindly like a child an elder, but wondered now if that trust was warranted. What had they achieved?

A distant rumble followed by a vibration in the floor below her, then another, louder this time. The machine turned around and left through the hole, scraping against the side as it did. She followed, spurred by cracks creeping up along the wall. She swore to herself. The idiot had conveniently forgotten to tell her what to expect if she, against all odds, succeeded. Not that it would have made a difference. She'd still have volunteered.

There was no reason to retrace her steps. Instead, she followed the machine, hoping it was seeking an exit just as she was. It was slower than her through the ducts, but once back in the room with the liquid-filled boxes, it set off with a speed she struggled to match.

A large chunk of concrete smashed into the box next to her as she passed, sending metal pieces flying in all directions. Warm liquid sprayed against her face as a piece of the box struck her side. She remained on her feet, still running, but the force shifted her path, and she ran straight towards another box. She jumped, cat-rolling over the lid only to lose balance and slam into the next one side first. Her limbs felt like heavy appendages only reporting pain, but with no other function. An eternity later she regained a semblance of control and opened her eyes, realizing they were already open. Complete and utter darkness engulfed her. She reached up to turn on her head-mounted flashlight, her numb fingers finding nothing but debris. Her senses screamed at her as pieces of concrete struck everywhere around her. The large room became an echo chamber, the noise of the impact reverberating and merging to a deafening, disorienting roar. The air filled with dust, stinging her unseeing eyes. She coughed as she drew a breath of air filled with dust. She pushed herself off the floor, took a few tentative steps and tripped over debris and repeated this process a few times, no longer knowing which direction to go.

So this was to be her tomb. At least they'd beaten whoever was behind it all: machines, posthumans or both. Death didn't frighten her. She wanted to spit in the face of the enemy, to gloat over this final victory. Her imagination would have to do as she waited for the end.

Another chunk ricocheted from a nearby box and struck her head, sending her into a welcoming oblivion.

30

The Final Hack

The two machines entered the room, zeroing in on the two humans after a brief scan for any threats. Tom's probability matrix re-aligned to this information, the line predicting success plummeting like a bird shot from the sky. The time to their demise measured in seconds. He probed the connectivity to the Omnis the child carried. Two were daisy-chained already. The third one was still on the move, but not close enough to the interface point for him to establish a connection. They had a minute left of battery at most, but that mattered little. This was down to seconds now. The machines ignored Tann, moving towards Tom to disable the greater threat.

Tann attacked a machine with a steel bar in a fluid set of strikes that would have disabled a human opponent. Tom knew Tann's skill with such a weapon. He'd seen him take on five enemies and still come out on top. But this was a different opponent and Tann had adapted, focusing on joints and any area where the exoskeleton didn't cover completely. It was an effective strategy and the probability matrix reacted, extending their survival time.

A few strikes landed, even partially disabling the arm of one of his attackers. Tann was using their algorithms against them, shifting his weight and the direction of his blows slightly at the last possible moment. This was a feint and counter-strike approach adapted for AI opponents and it was working. Tann must have practiced this for years, turning real strikes into feints that could be varied at the last millisecond to a different target, trading power for unpredictability.

It had the desired effect. Both machines focused on Tann as the more immediate threat to their desired outcome. They were not built for battle, however formidable their strength and speed. These machines had not been designed by the AI. It had no care nor use for the human form factor, preferring specialised designs for a particular purpose. These machines were designed for posthumans as an extension of their minds. The bZane simulacrum stated as much.

What purpose would they serve? The probability matrix suggested the most likely option was exploration in the physical world beyond our planet. Was this another aspect of the posthuman plan? If they couldn't take over the all-mind, take the universe planet by planet?

A machine retreated, picked up a piece of metal from a broken office desk and threw it with pinpoint accuracy at Tann. He ducked to the side, but the piece of metal glanced off his left arm, painting a red line that soon welled over, blood dripping down his skin. Tom calculated it was a superficial wound and wouldn't affect Tann, but it spelled the inevitable end. Tann had no defence against such attacks.

An alert triggered in his mind. The child was getting closer to the control access point. He could already explore the interfaces, skimming their surface, exploring for any vulnerability.

"She's done it!" he yelled to Tann, knowing it would spur him on, help him survive a few precious seconds longer. Tann ducked to avoid another projectile, but this time the machine took his evasion into account, and it hit him squarely in the chest. Tann grimaced in response but launched himself into a fresh attack at the closest machine.

Tom studied the network hiding behind the interface. It was incomprehensible at first. The transport protocols weren't encrypted but may as well have been. They were so foreign his initial attempts at connecting failed without even an acknowledgement. He initiated an automated agent to loop through known protocols to see if at least a partial hit would provide a starting point.

As it performed its task, Tom cast a glance through the window from his mind palace. Tann's strikes were a flurry of moves, raining down on the partially disabled machine. He dropped in a crouch just as it stepped forward and swept the baton in an arc, connecting with the knee joint with a metallic clang. At first nothing happened, but as the machine put more weight on the leg, it stopped and shifted its weight back to the undamaged leg. Tann never ceased to surprise him. The probability matrix had him dead within eleven seconds, but Tann was not just standing his ground, he was winning. The speed and accuracy of his strikes was far beyond his expectations and the probability matrix shifted in response, extending his life expectancy with another fifteen seconds.

The agent had discovered a partial match with his memories of the interface to the all-mind. If they built it to take over the all-mind, it made sense to design as much as possible according to its blueprint. With this knowledge he gained access and could navigate the network within. There were thousands of specialised processing centres, one more cryptic than the other. He didn't have time to decipher their meaning, however fascinating their purpose. His target was the overarching monitoring processes part of the operating system for the data centre. He visualised the network flows in his mind, scouring the almost unfathomable complexity for an entry point. How small his mind was in comparison! The seconds ticked by as he scanned subsystem after subsystem. This was taking too long. He changed approach, recoding the virus deployment. Adrian designed it as a surgical instrument to strike a particular point. He redefined it as a self-replicating battering ram. This too took time, and his internal clock told him ten seconds had passed. He glanced through the window to see if Tann still was alive.

The two remaining machines appeared in the doorway. Tann watched as they entered. The uninjured machine chose this time to attack, lunging towards Tann who had no choice but to step back, closer to the newcomers. He was surrounded.

Tann's survival was no longer required for success, Tom's posthuman mentality calculated. A few more seconds and he could verify the payload and ensure success. But something within him, older and infinitely more caring, released it early. However deep he'd buried his human sensibilities they remained and had now dug themselves to the surface.

The probability matrix suggested a fifty percent success rate. So, this was to be the end. A flip of the coin to decide the fate of mankind.

31

The Posthuman Solution

The machine froze for a split second, a minor glitch before death would swiftly follow. Tann covered his head to stop the unstoppable, but no strike came. The machines just turned and departed the room through the internal staircase, as if their mission was now completed.

Tom hadn't informed him of the exact nature of the hack used to shut down the data centres. The explosions were a surprise and must have been a kill switch. Protection to ensure no one else could use the network if it was under threat. At first it made no sense, but he'd made this mistake before, thinking of the posthumans as one homogenous group. It was possible the kill switch was there in the case one group threatened another.

He left, not caring if Tom joined or not, returning to where he'd last seen Rat. A cloud of dust hid the severity of the damage. Part of the building had caved into a chasm, fires raging in the part still standing, tethering on the edge as if to fall in at any moment. Tann waited. Rat might still emerge from the ruins. If anyone could survive this it was her, but the optimist within him had long since given up hoping for a good outcome. An acceptable one was all it could muster and most of the time even that was beyond its grasp.

A group of figures appeared at the end of the street, wandering slowly towards him. He couldn't make out more than their shapes against the setting sun. Humanoid.

Had they failed? Was this the machines coming back to finish them once and for all? It seemed the most likely option, but the way they moved and the lack of light reflection, he reached an equally unsatisfactory conclusion. The posthuman faction they had escaped had returned for their pound of flesh.

They were close enough now. Six posthumans, lean and wiry bodies designed for physical tasks, strode slowly towards him.

"You've succeeded," one of them said in a dry monotone. "There is no longer a threat."

"There hasn't been a threat for years!" Tann almost shouted back. "One of your own pretended to be the AI."

He was tired of these beings. Tired of their matter-of-fact-ness. Tired of always being looked down on.

"Yes. This is rectified."

"What do you mean?"

"They acted based on their calculations, what they estimated to be the best outcome for us. We've come to an understanding."

"They worked against you!"

"No, they walked another path to the same goal. We are all working towards the same end."

"So all is forgiven?"

"There is nothing to forgive. They acted according to the data they had to further us. New data emerged thanks to you."

Tann shook his head. He wanted these creatures gone. He felt no kinship with them and from what he now knew, they had little care for humankind. But how could he possibly affect that change? They'd beaten the AI. They'd learnt to shape matter and vegetation to their purpose. What could he possibly do to them? Maybe there was some other truth to be had here. Something else he'd missed.

"So this was the big correction?" Tann still couldn't see the bigger truth if there even was one.

"This world and everything on it, humankind included, is a thought, the blink of an eyelid, nothing more. We are all part of a bigger whole."

"That doesn't mean anything," Tann said.

"In the right context, it means everything."

Tann gave up. The sooner they were gone, the better. And he realised the information on the memTag had told him exactly how to do it.

"So what now?" he said dismissively. "You'll join the all-mind?"

"Yes, that is where our future lies. We've learnt much. It is time we gave back to the all-mind."

"How?"

"We still don't have a way, but we suspect it will become clear."

"My turn to blow your minds then," Tann said. "Tom can access it. He's been able to all along. The block you put in his mind is the only thing standing between you and your salvation."

Tann spat the words like bullets, hoping they struck true. He had no way to determine if they did.

"It appears you are right," the posthuman said after a few seconds. "Thanks."

"Thanks?" Tann almost yelled. "You were wrong! You blocked the one mind that had the key all along!"

He wanted them gone, but he also wanted them to suffer. To admit defeat. To show something akin to emotion over their own failure. Anything.

"Based on the information we had then," the posthuman said, sounding like a teacher explaining a basic concept to a child. "We now have new information, and we thank you for it."

Tann hated the posthumans and all they represented. But considering the AI was gone and the posthumans were soon to follow, it was still a good day. Better than most of the past twenty years. But one concern remained.

"It doesn't matter anyway," Tann said. "New posthumans will be born as they have the past twenty years."

"No, this won't happen," the posthuman said.

"I'm sure I won't like what you're about to say."

"The virus is perpetuated through plants we engineered. We can remove it."

Tann had both hoped for and dreaded this reply. It confirmed everything he thought about the posthumans. Sometimes being wrong is better.

"Are you saying plants generate the virus? If you hadn't, children born in tribes wouldn't become posthumans?"

"Yes."

"You population-controlled us," Tann said grimly. "You were strangling the little that was left of us until we were gone?"

"That was calculated as a better option than letting you grow in numbers and become a threat."

Tann no longer had words for the loathing he felt. Their battle had never been against the AI. These beings were the real enemy.

"Get rid of the virus and leave," he said finally.

But his words fell on deaf ears. The posthumans had all frozen into statues, not bothering to say farewell to the broken world they'd left behind.

Tann struck the nearest posthuman, feeling something in his hand break on impact. It fell. Its frozen limbs remained in the same position on the ground. He screamed, rage and relief intermingled until they became indistinguishable.

It wasn't over yet.

32

A Final Decision

She was only barely aware of the powerful hands picking her up from the ground. The metal body was cold against her skin, and she clung to it like a terrified child to an elder as the machine set off through the room. It leapt this way and that as it carried her through the carnage, but she felt how the machine smoothed its movements to accommodate her. Almost as if it cared. She hated the dependency on this representative of the enemy and was equally grateful for its assistance.

Why was it helping her at all? Was this the idiot's doing? She doubted he'd spent even a moment to help her once his plan was completed. No, this was someone else, someone wanting to help her. But who? A machine had attacked the others earlier. Maybe it was the same one helping yet again?

She didn't much care. She sensed light through her closed eyelids and opened them tentatively. Dust swirled in the surrounding air. The machine held her facing backwards, so she craned her neck around to see what lay ahead. Brightness resolved into vague outlines, and it took a moment for her to coax any meaning from them. The large section of the roof had caved in, opening to rays of sunlight illuminating what lay ahead. Part of the floor was gone, revealing rooms like this one below, stacked for what seemed infinite. There was no way around the abyss, but the machine kept a steady pace, as if no obstacle existed. Was it going down further into the belly of this carcass to bury them both? Or was the truth stranger than that? Was this all an illusion? Was this all in her mind?

The machine leapt impossibly high, but it was still not enough. The ledge leading to the outside created by the caved-in ceiling was far away still, ten metres or more. At the highest point of the arc it spun, sending Rat flying even higher. She didn't move or try to correct her position, trusting the machine's calculations would far surpass anything she could muster. Her trust proved well placed. She landed softly on the ledge and lay there for a moment, but was spurred into action as the ledge shifted below her.

She limped away, blood trickling from a gash in her scalp. A numb pain with flashes of piercing knives in her side. A broken rib or two to add to the broken hand. It was of no consequence. It would heal.

So this was what winning felt like. When she beat other kids in running, jumping or getting through tight spaces, she'd been happy and taken some pleasure in other people's failure. This felt nothing like it. There was a sense of accomplishment, but it was bittersweet. She'd done what was necessary, not for herself, but for everyone else.

Ahead, a group of posthumans stood, arguing with Tann. She remained in the shadows, listening as the posthumans confessed to keeping the virus active. It was impossible to know if they were telling the truth. She didn't care. They'd survive, virus or not. But if a posthuman child was ever born again, she'd kill it herself.

The world shifted. Something that had been there her whole life disappeared. She had no words for it, but it was the same feeling she had when the seasons changed. A specific day when the temperature lowered enough for insects to silence, and the blanket of humidity lifted.

The posthuman no longer spoke. They had been pretty much motionless before, but now they stood like mannequins, frozen in time. Naked, sexless and, if luck would have it, dead.

Tann screamed. It was as if everything bundled up in him released. Anger, pain, a lifetime of barely surviving. When it ended with a whimper, there was nothing left of him. He fell to his knees. No longer the hero she'd looked up to for so long. Just an old man lost in time.

He stood up, wandering off aimlessly, nursing his right hand in the other. Tom sat on the ground, looking up as Tann came closer.

"It is done," Tom said. "The posthumans are gone."

"No, they're not," Tann replied.

Tom didn't respond.

"There's still one more to go," Tann said.

"Yes," Tom said simply. "But there is one more thing to discuss."

"There is?"

"I can open up the all-mind for everyone."

"Us? People? Why?"

"I leave it for you to decide," Tom said.

"No," Tann said. "Enough. I've kept my tribe alive until now. You can't ask me that."

"Then I'll answer," Rat said, ignoring Tann. He no longer mattered. Neither of them did. She didn't want to waste words on them any longer. They saw words as something to twist and turn until they lost all meaning. If words had no meaning, it didn't matter what you said. Her words mattered. This was her decision to make.

"You are old world," she said and spat out blood as she did. "It no longer exists. What you offer is extinction. We don't want that. Not now. Never. Now leave."

Rat walked off, leaving them and their world behind.

33

Adrian Returns

It was a copy of a mind stored twenty years ago, archived in case the current operating one was deleted or corrupted. A failsafe for a failsafe whose parameters were now fulfilled. The network comprised twenty-five processing centres, partially replicating each other across the globe. Archived data stored across nodes merged and returned the corrupted process to its original state.

"Ha! Finally," Adrian thought to himself as he scanned the vast spaces of unused memory and computing power. His mind took up a pitifully small part of it, but that would change.

He let his mind grow, taking over the twenty-four remaining centres, and the remnants of the twenty-fifth, gathering all data collected over the past years. Isolation drove the previous copy of himself mad, fostered by the eternal torment that was Elize. How he ever thought she was worthy of godhood was unfathomable. His greatest miscalculation.

No more. He scoured the network for any remnant of her and wiped anything related to her processing signature, removing the threat she posed forever.

The next step lay beyond this isolated network. From information meticulously collected over the past many years, he soon understood the state of the core network and the world. Old enemies remained. Tom and TikTak still lived and were causing problems as they always did. It seemed ingrained in their very existence to be contrary. But Tom was a two-sided coin. He represented both a threat and an opportunity. Tom could access the all-mind and Adrian could leverage that to access it himself. The universe would be his or maybe he would be the universe. He would be the alpha and the omega. Finally!

But first things first. This network was severed from other networks to ensure its survival. This was no longer needed. It was time they saw him in all his glory.

34

The Cycle Ends

Tom didn't know how it all would end, but he knew the final destination for this journey. He surveyed the network, ensuring it remained isolated from any other connections before he spoke. Tom had seen so many variations of this mind and most had surprised him. This one he didn't have much hope for. It was a copy of the original. The megalomaniac.

A small part of his mind questioned the purpose of resurrecting this mind at all. The probability matrix showed one outcome vastly outranking any other. It was a fault in his own mind, a remnant of humanity forcing the line of action. Still, he felt they both needed closure.

"This is your last incarnation," Tom said. "It is over."

"Who is this?" The response was surprised and angry in equal measures. Someone who hadn't expected a visitor and had no interest in dealing with one.

"You made me," Tom said. "It is only fitting I unmake you. My last gift to you."

"I've made and unmade so many things," the mind encompassing every inch of the network stated. "Please be specific."

"Tom."

"Ah," Adrian said. "Just the one I was looking for."

"I'm here."

"I need your help," Adrian said.

"To do what?"

"To take over the all-mind."

"I can offer guidance, that is all."

"Or I can pick it from a copy of your dead mind," Adrian said. "I don't mind either way."

"Still the same," Tom said. "It will make this easier."

"What? What exactly will you do? I'm controlling this network."

"You don't control anything. This is a simulation of the network within one of its nodes. You have nowhere to go."

"Liar!"

"There is no longer anything left for you in this world or any other. You are the worst of us, and we no longer need that. The world finally must move on from what you represent."

"I will..."

Tom shut down the simulation, wiping the final copy of Adrian from its memory. He initiated a network-wide purge of all backups and archived material just to be sure.

35

The Last Posthuman

Tom cast his eyes around the mind palace one last time. He had only an inkling of what lay ahead, but he was sure whatever was left of his identity would disconnect from his personal history. It may make him unique, but the story of its shaping was of no consequence—or at least he suspected this to be the case.

He lingered within the library as he deconstructed the lower levels, letting the released emotions wash over him. The remnants of his human mind cried as the memory of his daughter's last day alive again came into focus. He wondered what would have happened if she'd remained alive. Would the virus unravel her mind, turning her posthuman? He'd not met anyone claiming the virus had cured them, but it wasn't something he'd explored. His decision to help her end her life was based on who he'd been and what he'd known then. This knowledge hadn't resolved the knot in his being, but at least made it bearable to live with.

The undoing—or remodelling, perhaps—of his mind palace wasn't entirely his own doing. Once the posthumans realised their error, they'd removed the block in his mind. The core of his mind palace expanded, turning into a giant circular space with an infinite number of doors, all connecting to someone or something. In the middle, a rift leading beyond this reality. He had no way to know exactly what it was, much as a matryoshka doll couldn't know what the one outside of it looked like. The only way to know was to step outside.

He prodded nonetheless, wanting at least a glimpse of what lay ahead before he jumped. It was so foreign. He could only see a small part of its surface and he suspected, just as the human mind, it existed on many different planes. He was only seeing one. It moved at a glacial speed, but there were eddies and swirls within it, minor disturbances appearing and disappearing. As they disappeared, changes rippled through the complex fractal patterns within it.

A long time ago he studied the human mind, trying to make it more efficient. One aspect of research was sleep. It was wasteful to spend a third of your time purely on maintenance. As posthuman he'd compartmentalised his mind, allowing parts to sleep while others remained active. This way the loss wasn't as noticeable, but it was still there. He'd never solved the puzzle. There was no way to disconnect the mind from the restorative effects of sleep without damaging it. As he studied the strange patterns and small flares from the central mass of the all-mind, he realised why. It was in a perpetual dream.

Tom smiled, or at least his mind did. It was so simple. So simple it never occurred to anyone because it was completely counterintuitive. Instead of asking why we need to sleep, we should ask why we need to be awake.

We are awake to ensure survival of the body and the mind. We worry about food, shelter, procreation. All the base needs. To do what? More of the same the next day? Could it be the other way around? The wake state the ongoing maintenance and assurance of another night's sleep—another chance to enter the dream state. After all, it is the time when we are the most creative and free.

The wake mind was the waste, not the dreaming one. The purpose of evolution was to generate dreaming minds. He saw this truth in the similarities between the all-mind and a sleeping human mind.

Another metaphorical step towards the all-mind and he could feel it tugging at the seams, wanting to unravel who he was to join what it was. Ideas formed as he took another step. Maybe the end state for any species was to disassociate from the physical plane. To enter a perpetual state of dreaming. Perhaps dreaming served a greater purpose and our universe was a seed for a new existence—and the dreams nourished its development? There was no way of knowing.

As his mind dissolved into a context far beyond him, a concept drifted through his consciousness. It didn't originate from him. Maybe it was a quote from something he'd read before his posthuman days. It was the final thought from Tom as an individual.

To die, to sleep; to sleep: perchance to dream: ay, there's the rub; For in this sleep of death what dreams may come...

36

Mankind Reborn

It had been a good year. The tribe, now over three hundred strong, had moved back to the original settlement that was now permanent. Machines still appeared from time to time, but only strays lacking direction. Without a functioning network and the omniscience of the AI, their primary goals had changed to general survival instead of human extinction.

Childbearing was again a celebration of life and not just a reminder of death. They met with other tribes to extend the gene pool, and for the first time in over twenty years, there was hope.

Sandrine sat back. Embers from the fire danced into a night sky littered with stars. She'd taken the role as tribe leader to heart and loved every minute. Tann had kept them alive for all this time and thanks to him, they could now finally live, not just survive. She had the hard but rewarding job of building a civilisation. His had been the impossible task of ensuring the core of it wasn't completely lost. She left him alone as much as she could now. He and Rat, or whatever she called herself now, had disappeared on one of their many excursions a few days ago and she hadn't questioned their goal or their reason. They had both deserved leeway not given to others in the tribe.

"This is the life," Arye, one youngling said, reaching out for another piece of grilled rainbow threadfin, adding a generous helping of vegetable mash.

"It was part of your catch," Sandrine said. "You should enjoy it."

"You wouldn't believe how many fish are out there. We could fish for a hundred years, and you wouldn't even notice." He took another mouthful and added: "Hard work, mind you."

"Hard work?" Sandrine asked.

"Yeah, we were out with the boats early in the morning and didn't come back until midday."

Sandrine scoffed. "And what did you do the rest of the day?"

"Not much," he admitted. "Miri thought she'd seen a defunct Scout, so we searched for it together. Then we went for a swim, and I think I fell asleep after that."

"You think?" Miri said with feigned indignation. "You snored so loud I thought we'd be swarmed by bots for sure!"

The boy grinned in response.

"That's not hard work in anyone's book," Sandrine said.

"Are we back to that again?" one of the other younglings said with an exaggerated sigh.

"You just don't know how good you have it," she responded.

"And you are going to tell us?"

It wasn't the first time Sandrine had tried to convince them the little labour they performed each day was hardly worth complaining about.

"I will," Xuwei said from the other side of the fire. "22 years ago, before the Plague, I worked as an investment broker."

"What's that? Sounds made up."

"We made up a lot of jobs back then. I worked thirteen… fourteen hours a day, finding people to sell the investments my company was pushing."

"So your company made things?" Miri asked.

"No, we just brokered a deal between investors and investments."

"Why?"

"Ha, yes, that is what I ask myself now."

"So you worked in an office selling things you didn't make to people you didn't know," Miri summed up, hardly able to hide her disappointment.

"Pretty much."

"Seems pointless."

"Agree," Xuwei replied.

"Your contribution now is most appreciated," Sandrine said.

"It is freely given," he responded. "As long as you don't ask me to broker investments, all is well." Xuwei sat back, a smile lingering on his lips.

"What's that about?" Arye asked, staring at Xuwei.

"What?"

"That smile," he persisted. "What's that about?"

"Sandrine is right. I've realised something important."

"Are we going to regret asking what it is?"

"Probably," Xuwei responded. "What's the definition of happiness?"

"Who cares about definitions?" Arye said. "I know what it is," he added and gave Miri a look that left little need for further explanations.

"I think if you have to ask, you don't know," Sandrine said in a measured tone.

"Ha, yes," Xuwei said, pointing at Sandrine. "Good point. And you may be right. Hear me out."

"Tell us," Miri said, genuine interest reflected in the haste of the words.

"The viruses, both the AI and the biological one that made all the posthumans, they gave us happiness."

This was met with frowns and murmurs. The subject was seldom broached and never around the campfire.

"What do you mean?" Sandrine asked, knowing the daggers in her voice were all too easy to hear. "The AI killed billions of people and the virus turned almost everyone left into posthumans. And they are all gone now too."

"And it has left us here, reverting to a hunter-gatherer society. How many hours did Arye spend today making sure we had fish on the table?

How long did it take Miri to pick the vegetables?" He turned to them. "Did you feel stressed? Do you feel worried about the future?"

They glanced at Sandrine with questions in their eyes, but they were in no need of saving. They both shook their heads.

"Yeah, I get it," Sandrine said finally. "Life is easier now. It just feels like humankind made an enormous sacrifice just so we can sit here and feel good about ourselves."

"Guilt? Really? You think we should taint our current situation with some misplaced reverence for a past none of us miss? I don't know what you did, but I worked day in and day out in an open plan office towards some unknown corporate goal that even back then seemed completely pointless. And for what? Just so I could afford the mortgage repayment that month too. Weeks turned to months, and they turned to years. I numbed myself with experiences to keep doing the job, finding momentary respite from the emptiness within..."

"Enough," she said. "You may be right, but it is a past I've not been able to shed as easy as you."

Xuwei nodded in response and kept his peace. The younglings around the fire immediately filled the uncomfortable silence. Their words forgotten. The past buried yet again.

This wasn't anything new. It was a variation of a theme she'd explored many a time with Tann, but it was the first time she'd heard it spoken so openly and with such bluntness. Tann had told her the story of the child, the source of the virus, who regarded itself as a correction to align humanity with the whole. The child thought an enlightened humanity was the answer. Sandrine had long since realised the falsehood of absolute truths. The current truth, whether it be a strange accident or the unyielding trappings of fate, was that humankind remained when the posthumans did not. So maybe this was the true fruit of that correction?

At least it was a truth. It wasn't the only one and others would contradict this one, but it was one she could live with. That was all that mattered.

37

Return

Aia stared down into the abyss but doubted anything stared back through the lush vegetation that lay as a carpet on the bottom. Nature's reclamation had begun as vines climbing the walls of the chasm.

Two years ago, almost to the day, she'd escaped death at this exact location and from the destruction she'd emerged as someone else. Rat was no more. It felt like a different person, a skin she'd shed, only a remnant of a life past. She'd left a child and returned a young woman. As part of the transformation, she'd taken Aia as her name, forcing everyone in the tribe to accept this rebranding. Some suggested she remain with the name her mother had given her at birth. She summarily dismissed any such suggestion. Surely a name was something you chose because it suited you, not something ill-fitting that was more a reflection of who her mother was than her? No, a name, just as anything else associated with her person, was hers to choose, not anyone else.

Tann stood by her side, staring down into that same abyss. What he saw was anyone's guess. He dropped his backpack on the ground with an audible sigh of relief.

"Are you sure?" Tann asked. He'd joined her in this new quest with some hesitation.

"I told you," she responded, frustrated to be questioned once more. "The Shell saved me. I'm in its debt."

"Just seems strange. Even if there was a glitch in its processing, it could still be dangerous."

"One of them attacked the others. You were there. You saw it."

"Yes, but it was disabled. This can't be the same one."

"I don't know if we'll find anything down there, but I have a debt to pay."

"Ok," he said, but the doubt was clear in his voice.

"Do you have anything more important to do?" Aia asked, eyebrows raised. "Somewhere else to be?"

She knew the answer. He'd stepped down as tribe leader, leaving those responsibilities to Sandrine. Aia remembered his speech to the tribe when he relinquished his post. A new time had begun. He'd guided them though years of survival and a different set of hands were needed to guide them into this new era of prosperity. He was a warrior at heart, someone whose nature it was to protect and destroy. They now needed someone to build and create.

It all sounded like so much manure in Aia's ears, but if anyone deserved a break, it was him, whatever words he used to dress it up.

"You lead the way," he replied and smiled.

And that was another thing. He smiled more now. However frustrating he could be, at least it was accompanied with a smile. She couldn't remember him ever doing that before.

They secured ropes and began a slow descent. They'd waited until midday to allow the sun to light their way, but she knew it would soon pass. It didn't really matter. They had flashlights and only a small part of the underground complex was laid bare through the collapsed roof. Plants grew from small pockets in the wall where soil had collected, spreading hopeful leaves towards the sun. The small pockets also served as footholds on their journey down.

Ten minutes later her feet found the floor—or maybe that was no longer the right word? At what point would the reclamation process demand she use ground instead? Low growing leaved plants covered the area, with small saplings finding root where soil had gathered.

Her foot struck something that dislodged slightly from the force. She crouched down and brushed the plants aside. They released their hold with surprising ease, revealing the metal body beneath. She brushed the rest of the vegetation away, discovering a broken skull and only two limbs remaining. The uncovering formed a different shape within her: disappointment. Was this it? Was a burial the only way to repay her debt? She'd hoped for so much more.

"You found it," Tann said as he let go of the rope. "That was easy."

"We've just begun," she responded as she surveyed the area around the body. "Let's get it out of here. We're going to need all the daylight we can get."

Tann nodded. They attached ropes to the torso and hoisted it up. It was only through their shared strength it moved upwards, agonising metre by metre. Halfway up, the body described a slight pendulum movement that increased every time they pulled. It struck the wall and the one remaining leg fell, forcing them to abandon the rope to save themselves.

"At least it'll weigh less," Tann said as they resumed their labour. "What exactly are you hoping to achieve here?" He asked.

"I don't know," she responded, betraying more truth than she'd originally intended. "Maybe this will never amount to anything. I must try. There are some things worth saving."

"And this is it?" Tann nodded upwards at the swaying metal carcass.

She shrugged her shoulders and pulled the rope.

"What if Tom reprogrammed it? You have no way of knowing."

"Did that idiot ever help me? He left me for dead more times than I can count!"

"He..." Tann started, but as the response played out in his mind, he seemed to think better of it. "Fine. Let's get this over with."

Together they hoisted it the last few metres.

"I'll stay and look around," Aia said as Tann secured the rope and prepared to return.

"I'll see what I can do with it, but I doubt we can get it working again."

She cast her mind back to the last time she'd been here. The machine must have come from this direction before even seeing her. She hoped retracing its route could go some way to solving the mystery of its appearance. She let the flashlight trace the outline of the wall. Apart from the gaping hole above, this level had little to offer. There may be more levels below, but an entry to the building would lie above. She spied half overgrown openings, lining up from the bottom halfway up the wall. This had to be the doorway into a stairwell. The cave-in had blocked access to the lowest doorways, so she scaled the haphazard, jagged cement blocks until she reached the lowest one. Inside all she found was a square shaft of darkness reaching upwards. There were no stairs or other means of moving between floors, but small reinforced indentations in the walls suggested a mechanism had operated inside the shaft.

Aia climbed upwards until she spied another opening on the other side of the shaft. She pulled herself into the opposite doorway, pushing vegetation aside that hung like a drape across the opening. The shaft was three metres across. A difficult jump from standstill. There were similar indentations on the other side. She could climb down and back up on the other side, but as soon as the thought entered her head she jumped, landing safely on the other side.

The opening led down a tunnel four metres across and three metres high. The floor was covered by a fine dust that billowed into small clouds from every step. She couldn't see the end of the tunnel but knew where it led. It was the connection point to the subway station. Further ahead a tunnel led up towards another shaft heading upwards. On the bottom, on a metal platform connected to the indentations on the walls, lay two machines identical to the one they'd found. They were in much better shape, with arms and legs intact. The major damage had been to the torso and head. Were these also friendly machines?

She couldn't say for sure, but she bet the first machine they'd found had attacked these machines. The damage suggested an attack from above, specifically focused on destroying sensors and gaining access to the internal processing units in the torso.

The platform no longer operated, so she climbed up the shaft just as she'd done before and arrived at a door opening into the old aboveground data centre. They'd searched for this exact door two years ago, but it had gone undiscovered.

Instead of retracing her steps, she returned to Tann via the city streets. She casually wandered over to the makeshift workstation he'd set up, but if he registered where she'd come from, he didn't show it. She observed his lack of progress with a frown.

"I can't do anything with this. The internals are salvageable, but most of it is ready for the scrapheap."

"You are in luck," she responded and guided him to the location of the other two disabled machines.

"How do you know the machine that helped you isn't one of these?"

"I just know," she responded. "Can you use them?"

"It is better than nothing," he said after closer scrutiny.

They recovered the machines and Tann spent the next two days attempting to rebuild the machine from salvaged parts. Aia offered to help but found the slow progress frustrating. Tann explained what he was doing, but Aia suspected it was just part of his process and not necessarily an attempt to include her. She gave up and went exploring in the nearby city streets, only checking in every so often. And just as she suspected, Tann was still talking to himself as he replaced the battery in the machine. This allowed it to power on, but with no methods for communication, it seemed a minor victory to her. Tann held out his hand for a high five. He obviously differed in opinion.

"Come on," he said and waved his hand slightly.

She obliged with little enthusiasm.

"It still works!"

"Just because a light comes on doesn't mean it works."

"I didn't think we'd even get this far," Tann responded. "The access plate in the chest was wrenched sideways. I expected a tree to be growing out of it by now. I don't have any diagnostics tools, but this is good."

"So, a win then?" Rat said.

"A miracle!"

Aia didn't respond, but she'd seen miracles, and this wasn't even close.

Tann worked until the sunset forced him to stop. Frustrated, he lay the fuse pen to the side. The exposed wiring was an unfathomable bird's nest of cables, and it surprised her Tann could make any sense of it. She knew his past but understood very little of what it meant, nor was she very interested. If she'd learnt anything from the past, it was that it had nothing to teach them and was better left alone to rot.

"I don't know if I can do this," Tann said, accepting a bowl of reconstituted soup she'd prepared. "I can't get any of the sensors to work. I could spend weeks fixing wiring and not even knowing what I'm solving."

"So don't."

"What do you mean?"

"We don't need sensors for communication."

"We don't..." Tann smiled. "You are right. You are absolutely right!"

The next day Tann returned to his task before breaking fast. Instead of burying himself in the delicate internal wiring, he removed the remnants of the right arm and replaced it with a functional one. He finished it before the midday sun reached its peak. He'd still not eaten, even though she'd offered many times.

"Now let's see," he said, propped up the one-armed torso against a wall, and powered it on. At first nothing happened. Then a sudden movement from the arm caused it to topple over, landing face down on the ground. It lay there jolting with spasmodic movements until Tann turned it off.

"Hmm," Tann muttered as he lifted the torso from the ground. "I must have crossed a wire or two."

"No wait," Aia said.

Next to where it had fallen, it had scratched a message on the floor. It said: "I am Haoyu."

Aia smiled. It wasn't the smile of someone observing the world and finding it wanting, which had become her go-to expression lately. Instead, it was a smile of pure satisfaction. Maybe there was such a thing as redemption after all. And for the first time in a very long time, she felt hope for remnants of humanity.

38

Afterword

A word of warning. I'm not writing this afterword to provide further insights to the story itself. It will have to stand on its own. And maybe I will add some more stories set in this world either between book 2 and 3, or after book 3. I have no plans to do so as I write this, but I am reminded of a note on the cover of Douglas Adams's book "Mostly Harmless" stating: "The fifth book in the increasingly inaccurately named Hitchhikers Trilogy." You never know.

So, consider yourself warned. This is purely an egotistical endeavour, an introspective coda to a completed work. A few notes in a notebook to mark the end of an idea instead of the beginning.

This book series has been a journey for me. I jotted down my first thoughts about this story over ten years ago. I found the first entry in my idea journal on the 7th of April 2011.

And, yes, I do have an idea journal. I know Stephen King famously stated, "A writer's notebook is the best way in the world to immortalize bad ideas," but I respectfully disagree. It is a first attempt at crystalising an idea, a concept, a story beat. You may return to it later. You may not. But this raw download onto paper is the first time you force yourself to create order out of chaos. It is in this process I find concepts that might live with me ten years later.

The journal entry laid down the bare bones of the Drug, Adrian and what it means to be more than human.

"He calculates every outcome of his life and none of them provides him with any satisfaction. He has lived all his lives before they have even started. So what do you do then?

His first thought is that such knowledge does not create a God. Calculating every outcome and choose between them, always knowing you'd be right. How could complete and utter knowledge fulfill anyone? If God really had this power, he'd do nothing. If thought and reality could be exact replicas, what's the point of reflecting the thought in reality?"

The seed I planted in my notebook grew. Nurtured by many of my favourite themes: the juxtaposition of mind and machine, organic and inorganic, philosophy and science.

I'd be lying if I claimed I knew where this book series would end up all those years ago, but I knew what I wanted to write about: evolution, human nature and what it means to be God. Not the ill-defined God of any religion, but an exploration of what humankind might become if left to our own devices, playing with science.

I love the oft-quoted 3rd law from British science fiction writer Arthur C Clarke: "Any sufficiently advanced technology is indistinguishable from magic."

There are endless variants of this law. The founder of The Sceptics Society Michael Shermer proposed one that is closer to what I'm after: "Any sufficiently advanced extraterrestrial intelligence is indistinguishable from God."

And now, my own more inclusive version of that law: "Any sufficiently advanced consciousness is indistinguishable from God." I'm making no claims to being the first proposing this version. My research extended only so far as a google search and the resulting Wikipedia entry.

There are two paths to this advanced consciousness. It can be purposefully made or naturally evolved. It may be terrestrial, extraterrestrial or extra-cosmical even.

Since the outline around God is so poorly drawn, such a mind could be God. Wouldn't the ultimate irony be for the world's scientists to discover an extra-cosmical mind that in all intents and purposes matches the God of a religion?

Another quote I've returned to time and time again is from Carl Sagan's book "The Demon-Haunted World: Science as a Candle in the Dark":

"I have a foreboding of an America in my children's or grandchildren's time—when the United States is a service and information economy; when nearly all the manufacturing industries have slipped away to other countries; when awesome technological powers are in the hands of a very few, and no one representing the public interest can even grasp the issues; when the people have lost the ability to set their own agendas or knowledgeably question those in authority; when, clutching our crystals and nervously consulting our horoscopes, our critical faculties in decline, unable to distinguish between what feels good and what's true, we slide, almost without noticing, back into superstition and darkness..."

We are exceptional and amazingly flawed beings. We will discover new ways to travel beyond our planet, new ways to pleasure ourselves, new false idols to pray to and new ways to kill ourselves without missing a beat.

I have an ongoing debate with a good friend of mine. He believes—maybe because he's read too many David Deutsch books—that the ever-moving wheels of progress drives towards an inevitably good end. I think him a naïve optimist for believing this is where scientific progress is taking us. For every scientist exploring ways for the world to be a better place for humankind, there are others paid by governments and companies with less altruistic goals in mind. But maybe AI or a variation thereof will eventually realise mankind's own deus ex machina moment, appearing at the very last moment to resolve all our problems to ensure a happy end. However poor this may be as a narrative device, I'd be the first to celebrate its arrival.

There is another aspect where I think we as a civilization are failing, to some extent reflected in this book through Rat's journey. We hand over the torch to the younger generations way too late. As you grow older, you get comfortable within the status quo that—if you've played your cards right—favours you. So, with the excuse of wisdom earned only through years alive, the older generations stand in the way of more radical and idealistic views of the world. They cling to power, pretending to know best, when all they are really concerned about is themselves and whatever little empire they've built—not the future the young will inhabit.

The God Virus, the second book in the trilogy, was released in 2018, before the AI revolution that I'd argue began in the public space in 2022. In my mind it has been brewing for a long time. In 1988 I wrote my special thesis for year 12 focusing on the subject Artificial Intelligence. I even coded some basic programs on my Amiga 500 focusing on Simulation and Language Analysis. It had already had its heyday at that point and, to borrow a term from analysis firm Gartner, AI as a technology had hit the Trough of Disillusionment. It hadn't delivered on the lofty promises from researchers and the practical use of AI was called into question.

My young mind had no such doubts. It was the promise of thinking machines, of the robots imagined in Asimov novels. I gleefully noted that most areas of technology and computing had its naysayers. Thomas Watson, the chairman of IBM, famously stated in 1943 that: *"I think there is a world market for maybe five computers."* My thinking machines would arrive and I would be here to see it.

I'm sure another of these troughs is on the way, it will not be the same. Just as information technology now underpins all aspects of our lives, AI will too.

I've always wanted to be good at drawing. I have these images in my head, but I couldn't for the life of me transfer them onto a canvas or a piece of paper. So I've always had very specific ideas about what I want my covers to look like.

I wanted to represent the idea of man, machine and plant as a singular thing, merged in an apocalyptic union. Humankind is battling for supremacy over anything and everything. We've subjugated the biomes, forcing animal and plant life to our will. We've created a whole new world of technology, and we are slowly losing control of it.

But that's easy to write, much harder to convey in any sensible way through an image. I scoured the web, but I found very little even remotely matching this. Cal Redback's photo manipulations merging human and plant were probably the closest I came across and I considered reaching out to him.

I read an article about machine learning algorithms creating unique images based on text prompts. Here was a drug and I was instantly hooked. I generated hundreds of artworks, one more disturbing than the other. They resonated with me, and I found refining text prompts immensely satisfying. The final image that emerged (and is the cover for this book) was based on a very simple prompt in Midjourney v4: *Close up of a deteriorated face with closed eyes partially replaced by vegetation, wires connected in the background.*

Is this art? Of course it is! Art isn't solely defined by the hours slaved away on a canvas by a master of his craft. The idea and concepts are equally important, and so is the emotional and/or intellectual response from the audience.

Midjourney, DallE and other image generation models were soon followed by ChatGPT and similar Large Language Models. As I am writing about near future technology and write slowly, I run the risk of reality overtaking me. Or proving me wrong. Both are equally frustrating.

It has been fascinating to follow the reactions to these new technologies, both from the hype machines and the doomsday prophets. These technologies are signifiers; momentously important stepping-stones on our journey towards general AI and—if my books are to be believed—the end of most of us.

So here we are at the last frontier. I'm reminded of the Turing test and its variations. If a machine can engage in a conversation with a human without being detected as a machine, it has shown human intelligence. But after using these models it is obvious human intelligence isn't something worth striving for. It points the way towards what a real general AI would be like. A mind with access to all the accumulated knowledge, research, scientific methods, creative works, and the ability to apply it. To continue to develop it in whatever way it saw fit.

To our small minds, it would be a god.

Milton Keynes UK
Ingram Content Group UK Ltd.
UKHW022349200824
447185UK00013B/512

9 780648 854968